VICKI SI

"*VICKI SILVER.* ~~~~~~
book! – The **VICKI SILVER** series has the **energy** of a teenager and the **sophistication** of a new **Agatha Christie**. As usual adult authorities are an obstacle, but a trail of clues will **keep readers turning pages.**

I particularly liked how each of the detectives takes a different suspect and these segments are juxtaposed for the reader in a way that makes us **active participants** in **solving the puzzle**. The ending – is **exciting and satisfying**.

But this series of mystery novels is a **franchise on the move** and this particular book **delivers even more** on its promise than the first one, *THE STOLEN GEM*. Great work, young detective crew. Full speed ahead!"

– BookReview.com, by John Lehman, author of *America's Greatest Unknown Poet: Lorine Niedecker*

"Great Mystery Series! Safe Reading! – This is the second book I've read in the **VICKI SILVER** series and I'm **very impressed** to say the least. Vicki Silver works with her friends to solve crimes all the while demonstrating **Christian values.**

In the book, *CRUISE CONTROL*, what is supposed to be a fun family vacation turns **topsy turvy** when Vicki and her friends find themselves in the middle of a very **unexpected case.**

I have **recommended** this series to many of my friends. **Mystery, suspense and narrow escapes** flourish in this sea bound tale. In addition to trying to figure out who done it, young readers also receive a little **nautical knowledge** and history facts along the way! *CRUISE CONTROL* will leave the reader **excited to turn the next page!**

Hats off to **Alissa Wood** who has the ability to give readers what they want while maintaining **wonderful values** and a **Christian influence.**"

– Rene' Morris, author of *The Sonshine Girls*

Be sure to read all of the

VICKI SILVER

M Y S T E R I E S

Book 1 – The Stolen Gem

Book 2 – Cruise Control

coming soon

Book 3 – Hoofbeats

Book 4 – Fashion Conscious

Book 5 – Express Theft

Book 6 – Technical Difficulties

A hand reached inside and suddenly the lights in the room switched off. Vicki and C.J. turned around quickly to see the shadow of a man standing in the doorway.

The darkness concealed his features, making it impossible to identify him. But, there was just enough light silhouetting the intruder to clearly see the shape of a gun ... and then he pointed it in their direction!

VICKI SILVER

MYSTERIES

CRUISE CONTROL

ALISSA WOOD

Text Copyright © 2007 Alissa Wood
www.alissakwood.com

Illustration Copyright © 2007 Summertime Books
www.summertimebooks.com

Cover Design by Daniel Huenergardt
www.dhbookcovers.com

Published by:
Summertime Books
P.O. Box 79684
Saginaw, TX 76179

www.summertimebooks.com

ISBN-10: 0-980-18611-0
ISBN-13: 978-0-980-18611-6

CONTENTS

1. Bon Voyage...................................... 9
2. Man in the Black Tuxedo.................... 25
3. On the Case..................................... 36
4. The Assailant................................... 46
5. Captive... 56
6. The Hunt... 61
7. The Evidence................................... 64
8. The Chapel...................................... 74
9. Dark Hours...................................... 80
10. Door to Door.................................... 85
11. Suspect Number One......................... 94
12. It's Official! 101
13. Halifax, Nova Scotia..........................110
14. Attempted Escape..............................124
15. Quarantine...................................... 126
16. Intruder.. 132
17. Kidnapped...................................... 139
18. Missing in Action..............................143
19. Moments from Freedom......................147
20. A Crook in a Dinghy..........................156
21. Exoneration..................................... 164
22. Reunion..167
23. Forever...171
24. Two Tickets to Paradise......................175

CHAPTER 1

Bon Voyage

*"It seems that I'm forever missing you,
though you're not that far away.
I never have anything to do
when you're not here today."*

Although the radio was playing one of Vicki and C.J.'s favorite songs, Vicki was growing impatient, and turned it off.

"Come on," Vicki sighed as she honked the horn, peering past C.J. through the passenger side window. C.J. at seventeen, had short, dark brown hair and brown eyes.

Vicki's long brown hair was pulled into a ponytail and she brushed the stray strands from her blue eyes, which looked impatient as she stepped out of the car and stood to her height of five foot eight.

She was waiting for her friend, Catlin Stage, to arrive. Vicki was determined to be on time, especially considering their plans. She was tempted to walk up to the door and drag her friend out when Catlin finally emerged.

Vicki expected this, but was still frustrated. She knew Catlin tended to be fashionably late, so Vicki thought it best to pick Catlin up herself, for that very reason. She glanced at her watch and was relieved to see that they could still get to the dock before their scheduled departure.

Vicki sat back down and started the air conditioner, as it was eighty-five degrees outside – which was extreme for Sport, Maine. If it wasn't for the fact that Vicki was leaving her vehicle at the dock for the week, she would have kept the top down. Vicki watched as Catlin approached the red convertible.

Vicki, her family, and her friends, were all going on a cruise in the North Atlantic. They were looking forward to a week of seeing new things, and enjoying cooler temperatures. It would be the perfect vacation away from all of their hard work.

The ship is called the "Crystal Palace", named after the famous building in England. They were taking the New England tour, and one of their stops would be at Halifax, Nova Scotia – which is translated "New Scotland".

The brochure that their travel agent gave them boasted of beautiful scenery along the coast. Halifax is a town both rich in history and culture. There were said to be numerous clubs and cafes, along with a boardwalk filled with specialty shops. And that was just the beginning of their list of expectations.

They were also going to stop in Quebec City, Quebec. Quebec City, which is the Capital of the Canadian Province of Quebec, has been called the most French town outside of France. Since Vicki and her friends had never seen France, they thought this would be the next best thing.

Vicki pulled out the cruise map to remind herself all the things they would be seeing:

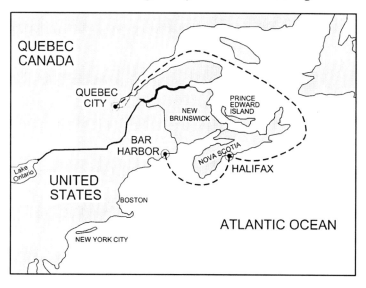

Vicki's friends, Joe and C.J., were already in the car. Joe, at eighteen, was six foot with blond hair and green eyes.

The return to High School was only a month away and this seemed like their last chance to have fun. A cruise would be the perfect getaway for the four friends, and they were anxious for their adventure to begin.

"I'm so sorry," Catlin said, scrambling to get through the car door. She was sixteen and had pretty black hair and brown eyes. "I forgot to pack some things." She pulled her three suitcases inside, setting two on the floor and pulling the other onto her lap. With the added passenger, and additional luggage, the backseat was becoming a bit crowded.

"Catlin," Vicki asked, "This is a one-week cruise. Why do you need three suitcases?" She looked back at her friend.

"You don't expect me to leave all my outfits at home do you?" Catlin asked with a look of mock surprise, and just a bit of a telling smile.

"I wish you would," Vicki commented, "We might be able to get to the dock a little faster if your stuff wasn't loading down my car." Catlin made a face at Vicki and turned away. Still, Catlin had a smile on her face. She was used to Vicki's teasing. Catlin was dedicated to her fashion, whereas Vicki and the others weren't quite as hung-up on the latest styles.

"This is going to be fun," C.J. said with a grin, "Just a week of fun and relaxation, and no cases to solve." Even though they were still teenagers, the group of friends had helped investigate several cases over the summer. They were glad to have a break from the stress of chasing down criminals.

"Sounds good to me," Joe remarked, "but don't count on it being too quiet. You girls are always getting involved with some type of mystery."

"I hope that's not the case this week," Vicki stated, giving Joe a look that clearly said that she was afraid just saying it aloud would jinx the entire trip, "That last investigation was hard work. We need to relax a bit."

Vicki drove down an inland highway heading for their coastal destination. The three hour road trip was one of the longest Vicki had ever driven on her own. The route took the group through Lewiston, Augusta, Bangor, and eventually to their launching point, Bar Harbor.

As they approached the dock district, the group could see the enormous vessel waiting for its passengers in the distance. The car wound its way through the various streets and around numerous warehouses, momentarily blocking the view of the awaiting cruise liner, until finally the group pulled up to the berth of their ship.

Once the group saw the monstrous ship up close, they could only stare in awe. The name, 'Crystal Palace', was etched across the bow of the stark white vessel. It stood some thirteen stories tall and was at least the length of three football fields.

Vicki pulled onto the dock and waved when she saw her family, who was already waiting. The teenagers piled out of the car and joined the rest of the Silver family. "Sorry we're late," Vicki said, eyeing Catlin with a playful grin, "We got a little held up."

"You're here just in time," her mother, Marie Silver, spoke up, "The ship's leaving in a few minutes. Let's get on board." Vicki's sister, Becky, looked over at her. She was not happy that Vicki had cut it so close, and because she was getting attention by making everyone wait. Vicki ignored Becky's look of utter annoyance.

It seemed that Vicki and Becky could never get along. Becky was nineteen and had long blond hair and green eyes. And, she was even more into fashion than Catlin.

Vicki's family, and the group of friends, walked up the gangway and boarded the ship. They immediately entered an orientation meeting. The crew highlighted all the activities on the ship, and discussed the schedule of events. A crewman handed out this card.

Welcome to the *"Crystal Palace"*
Please familiarize yourself with the ship's terminology and all emergency procedures.

Nautical Terminology
Aft – Rear or stern of ship
Bow – Forward part of the ship, front
Port – Left (note both words have 4 letters)
Starboard – Right
Stern – Rear (same as Aft)

Emergency Procedures
1. If the call for abandon ship is made, locate and don life vest immediately. Proceed to Emerald Deck.
2. Do not inflate life vest unless you are instructed, or you enter a lifeboat or the water.
3. To inflate, pull down on tabs located on vest. If this fails, inflate by mouth using tubes.
4. Only crewman may operate lifeboats, await their instructions.

Everyone on board had to attend a lifeboat drill and learn how to use a life vest. Vicki simply wondered when her vacation would start.

Once orientation was complete, the group looked around to find their cabins, which they found on the Aloha Deck. Joe got a room to himself and the girls shared the two cabins on either side. Vicki and Becky had seen enough of each other the past seventeen years, and decided to take separate rooms. Vicki would share a cabin with C.J., and Becky would bunk with Catlin.

The small rooms had two beds and a single dresser. There was a single chair at a small desk as well. At least they had a window.

Vicki and C.J. began to unpack their luggage, when an announcement came over the speaker in their room. "Attention, would Mr. Steve Garcia please report to the Wedding Chapel on the promenade deck. Mr. Garcia to the chapel, please."

The girls found the announcement quite interesting, but they would not allow themselves to be distracted from starting their vacation. After the interruption, the girls decided to take a walk around the ship. They thought a good way to explore the ship would be to climb to the uppermost deck and then work their way down. By the time they reached the top, they realized just how big the ship was, and how many people were on board.

The uppermost deck was called the Sky Deck and only had a small observation area. The next deck down was the Sport deck. It was comprised of two sections, one at the aft of the ship and another at the Bow. The aft section held a Rock-Climbing wall, several shuffle board areas, and two hot tubs. The other section, at the bow, was for the golf and tennis enthusiasts.

The next deck down covered the entire ship, from Bow to Stern, and it was called the Sun Deck. It held a swimming pool, a beauty parlor, and a large gymnasium.

The deck below that, the Lido Deck, had two more pools, a large sun terrace, and a dance club. The pools on the Lido Deck were larger than those on the Sun Deck, and deck chairs lined all sides. The decks and restaurants were bustling with visitors.

It would seem all the passengers had decided to explore the ship at the same time, and there were people walking back and forth throughout all the levels.

"This is so cool," C.J. finally said, in amazement, "I've never seen anything like this. And there are so many people."

"Me either," Vicki agreed, "I can't wait to check out the rest of the ship. This is so cool. We can spend all week just exploring this place, and having fun. We can go swimming, play games, and I don't want to miss going on the rock-climbing wall." Vicki continued, "This is great. We can finally leave all the mysteries behind."

"Yeah," C.J. remarked as the girls got caught in a throng of people making their way across the deck. Just then, the girls were pushed back as a man in a black tuxedo forced his way past them. He appeared to be in a hurry. He kept looking behind himself while he pushed through.

"You sure see some interesting people here," Vicki commented, watching the man as he passed. "Now that guy needs to relax. Doesn't he know he's on vacation?"

Vicki continued to watch the man as she and C.J. walked in the direction of the dance club. Vicki thought she saw something drop from the man's pocket. She turned and made her way through the crowd in his direction, but then her foot hit something and sent an object skidding across the floor. Making her way to where the object stopped, Vicki kneeled down and picked it up. It turned out to be a small jewelry box that was covered with dark blue velvet.

"Don't pay any attention to people like that," C.J. said, not noticing that Vicki was no longer with her, "Just relax and have fun."

Vicki spotted the man as he stepped through a doorway into the next room. "Sir, you dropped something!" He apparently didn't hear her, as he didn't so much as pause to look back. The crowd made it impossible to catch up with the man.

Vicki looked at the small box in her hand, and out of curiosity turned it over, wondering what was inside. She could no longer see where the man went in the crowd. She knew she would have to find him somehow and return the box.

She decided to open the box and see if there was anything to identify the man. Instead, she found a gleaming gold ring adorned with sapphires and diamonds.

There were initials engraved on the inside of the ring. It read, 'SG + SM + G = 4E'. Vicki couldn't imagine what they meant.

C.J. finally turned around to see that Vicki was on the Starboard side of the deck. She crossed through the crowd to join her. As she walked up, she said, "What's that?"

Vicki showed C.J. the ring before explaining how the man that had pushed passed them had dropped it. "I opened it to see if his name was in it. There is a ring but nothing to identify the owner."

C.J. replied, "Maybe we'll run into him later and we can return it. For now, just hang on to it and we'll worry about it later. There's still a lot of ship to explore."

Vicki shrugged, but continued to wonder. She could tell that C.J. was curious about the mysterious man and his ring, but didn't want to interrupt her vacation to hunt him down.

Both girls were startled from their thoughts by the boisterous sound of a horn. It was the signal that the ship was about to get underway. Neither girl knew what to expect next. They hurried to the railing to watch as the ship slowly began to move. It was almost imperceptible at first, but their queasy stomachs confirmed the motion.

They set their feet apart, one in front of the other, in order to steady their stance. Once they felt secure, Vicki and C.J. again directed their attention to the passing dock and shouted in celebration with the rest of the crowd. They found themselves waving at strangers that reluctantly waved back.

After looking around a while, and allowing their legs to get used to the rise and fall of the 'Crystal Palace', Vicki and C.J. made their way back down to the Aloha deck. They knocked on Joe's door, and he answered quickly.

"You've got to come and see this place," Vicki told him, "There is so much to do on the ship, and we've only seen a little of it so far. Want to look around with us?"

"Why not?" Joe said as he stepped out of his room, "It's too quiet down here anyway. Let's go." He followed them up to the Lido Deck and looked around, "You were right. This ship is huge, and look at all these people."

"Joe," Vicki said, "When we were up here earlier, we saw something strange."

"Don't tell me," Joe said, holding out his hands, "If it's about some mystery, I don't want to hear about it." He stopped as he saw the dance club, "What do you say we go check it out?"

He led them inside. C.J. followed behind them. Her boyfriend hadn't been able to make it. He was out camping with his family.

The club was packed mostly with older passengers, but a few teens were on the floor as well. They found a booth at the back and sat down. Soon, a blond waitress came to the table. Her nametag read "Natasha".

"Three sodas?" Joe asked Vicki and C.J. They nodded in agreement and he ordered. Their drinks soon arrived and they talked for a little while. Vicki's mind continually returned to the hurried stranger that had walked past them earlier. She thought he might have been headed for one of the restaurants.

After awhile, Vicki stood up to leave, "Where are you going?" Joe asked her.

"I'll be right back," Vicki said as she left.

Joe looked at C.J. for an answer, "Don't look at me," she replied with a shrug, "I don't know what she's up to."

Vicki walked out of the club and turned left. She walked towards one of the restaurants the man may have entered. Even though she wasn't on a case, her curiosity was getting the best of her. She was startled when a man stepped in front of her and asked, "Do you have a reservation?"

"Uh, no, sir," Vicki replied. "I was just looking for someone. Do you mind if I take a look around?"

"Certainly not," he replied, "Go right ahead."

"Thank you," Vicki responded and stepped into the dining room.

Vicki peered around the busy restaurant. Passengers of all types were seated at booths and tables. But, one passenger in particular stood out. He was the only one with a black tuxedo on. Vicki was sure he was the man who dropped the jewelry box.

She pulled out a pair of sunglasses and wandered over in the direction of the man. She found an inconspicuous place to hide out, and watched the man intently.

The man in the tuxedo didn't do anything out of the ordinary. He was sitting by himself at a table in the corner. Vicki watched as he ordered something to drink and looked around. Vicki casually walked over and sat at a nearby table. "May I help you," a waiter asked her.

"Yes, could I have a menu please," Vicki answered. The waiter obliged, and Vicki said, "It'll take me a minute before I'm ready to order. Thank you." As the waiter walked away, she held up the menu and peered over it to watch the man. He glanced around the room nervously, looked at his watch, and then tapped his fingers on the table.

Vicki decided to approach the mystery man and ask if he were missing a ring. But, just then, someone walked past his table. Vicki saw the man discreetly leave a note on the table as he walked by. The man in the tuxedo quickly read it and then left the restaurant. Vicki stood up and followed.

Again, Vicki was blocked by the maitre d'. "Did you find your friend?" he asked. Vicki shook her head, "No, but thank you." She quickly stepped past the maitre d', and out the door. But, the man was no longer in sight. Frustrated, she decided to return to the dance club and made her way over to her friends.

"Hey guys," she said as she sat down, "I'm sorry that took so long." Vicki didn't explain her short disappearance. She didn't want to admit to entertaining her curiosities.

"Sure," C.J. said slowly, "Why don't we get out of here? I want to look around some more."

"You go ahead," Joe told her, "We'll stay here. Is that okay with you?" He turned to Vicki.

"Absolutely," Vicki answered and stepped out of the booth so C.J. could get out.

Vicki said, "We'll see you later, C.J."

"Okay, I'll catch up with you later, C.J. replied.

Vicki sat back down and faced Joe, nervously twiddling with the golden cross necklace that hung around her neck, "What would you like to do next, Joe?"

"Would you care to dance?" he asked her, standing up. Vicki looked up at him, and smiled as best as she could.

"I don't think so. You know I'm not very good," she told him, "Everyone will be staring." She looked out the entrance to see the man in the tuxedo walk in. Quickly standing up, Vicki said, "On the other hand, I'll accept."

"Vicki," Joe whispered, "Are you going to take those sunglasses off?" Vicki had completely forgotten that she had left them on. She took them off and set them on the table.

Vicki led Joe to the front of the dance floor where she would have the best view of the stranger. "Why are we way over here?" Joe asked her.

"I want to be close to the door," she answered. "If I totally embarrass myself with my dancing, I want to be able to make a quick exit," Vicki said with a smile. Joe just shrugged his shoulders.

Vicki now had a clear view of the man. He was around thirty, she guessed, with brown hair.

He glanced around nervously again before sitting at a table by himself. A few seconds later, another man entered and joined him. It was the same man who had left him the note.

Vicki watched as the two men talked quietly for a few minutes. She led her dance partner closer so she could hear what was being said. Joe felt a little awkward giving up the lead, but tried to keep up. Vicki listened as the second man said, "We need to work this out right now. It can't wait any longer."

"I've already told you," the man in the tuxedo replied, "I didn't take the money."

"You're the only one who had access to the accounts that were skimmed," the second man continued, "If you're not responsible, then who is?"

"Look, I can't do anything about it now," the first man told him, "As soon as we get back to the offices, I'll go over everything. I'm sure I can figure out who is responsible."

Vicki became aware of a figure sitting at the neighboring table. He was obviously listening in on the conversation between the two men. When the man in the tuxedo mentioned finding who was responsible, the figure straightened up in his seat and began to rock back and forth nervously. From behind the partition, it was difficult to make out any distinguishing characteristics of the man who was listening in. It was anyone's guess who he was.

The second man stood and walked away before the man in the tuxedo could protest. Vicki watched as he sat silently for a moment. She couldn't help feeling sorry for the man. He didn't seem to know what to do next.

Vicki and Joe continued to dance while she wondered about what she had just witnessed. The man in the tuxedo stood up to head for the door but had to pass through the dance floor to get to it. The man ran into Vicki and Joe, literally. All three of them lost their balance and became a tangled pile on the floor!

CHAPTER 2

Man in the Black Tuxedo

The man picked himself up hurriedly and left without saying a word. "Hey," Joe called after the man in an angry voice, "Aren't you going to apologize to my girlfriend?"

"Joe, that's O.K.," Vicki said. "He's the same guy I was trying to tell you about. He bumped into C.J. and I earlier, and dropped a jewelry box. He seems to run into people a lot."

Joe stood up and helped Vicki to her feet. "Are you okay?" he asked, taking her hand. He looked at her worriedly. "That guy was really rude."

"I'm fine," she managed to say, "I'm just a little out of breath, that's all." She looked at the crowd that had begun to stare. She motioned that she was fine and they returned to their dancing. "Let's go now."

She picked up her sunglasses and walked out with Joe behind her. "Joe," Vicki said. "I think I just want to go back to my cabin for now. But, let's take the elevator. I'm a little too winded to be taking the stairs." Joe escorted Vicki back to her room.

As Vicki entered the room, she saw that C.J. had returned as well. She said, "C.J., I'm back. What have you been up to?"

"Nothing much," C.J. looked up from the magazine she had been flipping through, "You're back pretty soon. What happened?"

"Well, I would tell you, but you probably don't want to hear," Vicki replied. After a short pause, she continued anyway, "That guy in the tuxedo showed up again."

C.J. interrupted, "You're right, I don't want to hear about it. I'd rather read my magazine."

Vicki sat down beside her friend and looked over her shoulder, "What magazine is that?"

"It's from the Crystal Cruise Lines. It's a magazine all about the ship," C.J. answered. "Here, take a look at these maps of the ship."

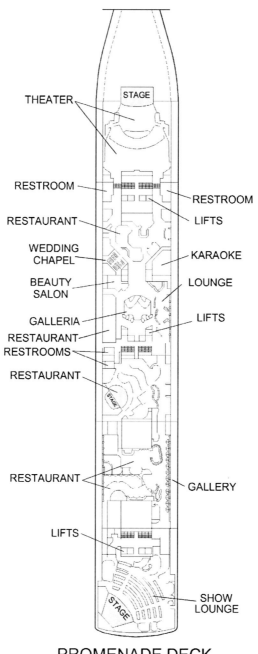

THEATER

STAGE

RESTROOM

RESTROOM

RESTAURANT

LIFTS

WEDDING
CHAPEL

KARAOKE

BEAUTY
SALON

LOUNGE

GALLERIA

LIFTS

RESTAURANT
RESTROOMS

RESTAURANT

STAGE

RESTAURANT

GALLERY

LIFTS

STAGE

SHOW
LOUNGE

PROMENADE DECK

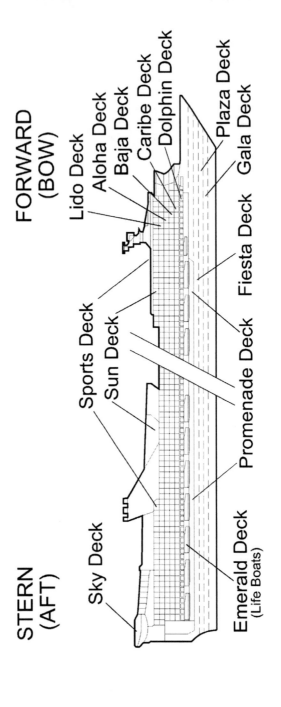

FORWARD
(BOW)

Lido Deck
Aloha Deck
Baja Deck
Caribe Deck
Dolphin Deck
Plaza Deck
Gala Deck

Fiesta Deck

Sports Deck
Sun Deck

Promenade Deck

STERN
(AFT)

Sky Deck

Emerald Deck
(Life Boats)

C.J. continued, "Vicki, did you know there's an arcade on the Sun Deck?"

"Really? How did we miss that?" Vicki responded, "Want to go check it out?" C.J. nodded and stood up. But, before she could open the door, someone knocked. It was Joe.

"Vicki," he asked, "We need to talk." Vicki opened the door, and Joe stepped in. He looked at C.J. as if to say 'Will you leave us alone for a minute?' C.J. got the message, "Vicki, I'll see you at the arcade," and left.

"I know what you were doing in the dance club," Joe said and smiled.

Vicki smiled back, "I knew I couldn't fool you. Did you hear what that man said?"

"Yeah, I heard," Joe said, "I should know better than to think there wouldn't be a mystery. You run into a case everywhere you go. What do you think he was talking about?"

"I'm not sure," Vicki answered, then paused in thought, "It sounded like they were talking about money."

"Maybe he owes some gambling debts," Joe pondered, "There is a casino on the Fiesta Deck."

Vicki shook her head slowly. "No, that doesn't sound right," she replied, "I wouldn't think there has been enough time to run up a large gambling debt."

"What do you think we should do," Joe asked.

"Nothing," Vicki answered, "This isn't really a case yet. Let's wait and see if it turns into something. I'm going to go meet C.J."

Vicki went up to the Sun Deck and found C.J. in the game room. The room was covered in arcade games of all sorts.

"Cool," Vicki exclaimed, as she saw one of her old favorites, "It's been forever since I've played this game. We've been pretty busy with all our cases. Let's play it together." Vicki lowered her voice and said, "By the way, I need to tell you something."

Vicki and C.J. stepped up to the game, and the two girls started playing. While their voices were drowned out by the noise of the game, Vicki told C.J. about the weird conversation she had overheard. "Well, what do you think?'

"I knew you couldn't resist checking out that guy in the tuxedo. I thought this was going to be a real vacation." C.J. shook her head in exasperation, but was still smiling. "That's okay, though. It sounds like someone needs to check it out."

"I'm glad I did," Vicki replied, "I found out something at least."

"Too bad we can't do anything about it, though," C.J. bit her bottom lip as she hit a button to blast an enemy.

"What do you mean?" Vicki asked, finally drawing her eyes away from the screen.

"Well," C.J. stated, "We don't know anything about this guy. We don't know his name or even what cabin he's staying in."

"I guess I can't just walk up to him and ask for his name and room number," Vicki nodded in agreement. "But, we know someone who can."

C.J. looked at Vicki knowingly, and said, "We could get Catlin to help. She might be willing to approach the guy and get some information."

"If we know anything about Catlin, it's that she has the confidence to approach anybody." They both laughed. C.J. and Vicki constantly kidded her about it.

"It's worth a shot," C.J. said, "She would at least have the confidence to ask his name. I think she would do it. She hasn't had a chance to help out much with our other cases."

The game reached its end, and the two girls headed for the Aloha deck. They reached Catlin and Becky's cabin and knocked on the door.

Unfortunately, Becky answered, "What do you want baby sister?" Becky used Vicki's least favorite nickname.

"Catlin," Vicki called through, "Can I ask you something." Catlin appeared at the door, and stepped into the passageway. Becky shut the door behind her. "Would you be willing to get some information about someone onboard?"

C.J. explained further, "Yeah, like introduce yourself to him, and see if you can find out who he is, or just anything about him at all." Catlin instantly turned on a smile.

"No problem," she said, "Just show me where he is and I'll talk to him." Vicki and C.J. laughed.

"We need to find him first," Vicki said, "Let's go look around. We're bound to find him. He's wearing a tuxedo and has brown hair."

Vicki, Catlin, and C.J. searched the ship from top to bottom, but found no sign of the man. They met back at Vicki's room. "Weird," Vicki said, "He has to be onboard. He couldn't have just disappeared."

"Something is going on here," C.J. agreed, tapping a finger on the desk, "And I plan to find out what it is. Looks like we can't use you after all, Catlin. At least not for now."

"It's okay," the sixteen-year-old said, "I can find someone else on the ship to investigate." Vicki and C.J. laughed again.

"Let me know when you find Mr. Tuxedo," Catlin said, "I'll do what I can once you find him." She walked off. Vicki and C.J. looked at each other, shaking their heads.

"Okay then." C.J. finally said, using her hands to push herself up, "Let's search the ship again, from bow to stern. Maybe we missed him in the crowd."

"It's worth a shot," Vicki nodded, "I'll start on the Sky Deck and you take the Gala deck. Let's meet back here and compare what we find, if anything." Her friend agreed and they left to search the decks again.

After working her way down, Vicki checked every inch of the Lido deck. She went back to the restaurant and looked it over, thinking that he might have returned, but there was no sign of him. The dance club held no sign of him either, as well as anywhere on Lido Deck.

C.J. looked into all the game rooms, theaters, and arcades that she could find, but doubted he would be in any. According to Vicki, he was around thirty. He wouldn't be anywhere near an arcade game. Her hunch proved correct and she met up with Vicki back at their room.

"I didn't find anything," C.J. reported, and got the same negative answer from Vicki, "He must be in his room. Where else could he be?"

"Maybe we should ask my parents about this," Vicki said softly, then shook her head, "I couldn't ask them. They would say I'm supposed to be on vacation, and not chasing wild hunches."

"But, maybe we should," C.J. said, "They might be able to help. "

"All right," Vicki gave in. The girls were heading in that direction when they saw a ship's steward knock on the door of one of the staterooms. It slowly opened at his touch.

The steward looked in the room and then stepped back. He then closed the door and ran down the hallway.

"Let's follow him," C.J. suggested, "It could have something to do with this case."

They followed the steward through the hallways, and up several flights of stairs, until he stopped at an office door. He knocked quietly and a loud voice said, "Come in." The steward stepped inside, leaving the door partially open. Vicki and C.J. crowded in front of the door, eager to overhear any information.

"Yes, steward. What do you want," a man asked. Upon reading the nameplate on the door,

Vicki concluded the voice was coming from the Captain.

"Sir," the young man said, "I went to Mr. Garcia's room, but he wasn't there. His door was open, but he was missing."

"He must have gotten off the ship before we got underway," said the Captain.

"I don't think so, sir," the steward replied, "His things were still in his room."

"All right then," the Captain continued, "Ask the crew if anyone has seen him."

The steward opened the door, surprising the two girls. "Excuse me. Is there something I can do for you ladies," he eyed them suspiciously.

"We couldn't help but overhear," Vicki started, "The man who's missing, what does he look like? Do you know?"

The steward replied, "It's a problem that involves one of our guests, and we really can't talk about it. This is a problem for the crew to investigate."

"If it's who we think it is, we've seen him several times since we came on board," Vicki said, "We ran into him, quite literally, in several areas of the ship. So, if you wouldn't mind, I would like to know if it's the same man."

"Well, he's medium height, in his late twenties, early thirties," the man replied.

"Do you have any other description?' C.J. asked.

"He also has brown hair, that's all I know."

"Did he have on a black tuxedo," Vicki asked.

"Yes. As a matter of fact, he probably was wearing a black tuxedo," the steward said in surprise.

"Sounds like the same man we saw," Vicki said.

"According to my friend here," C.J. continued, "He was talking to another man at the dance club. They were having an argument over money. Mr. Garcia, if that's his name, said he wasn't responsible, or something like that."

"And we think his disappearance might have something to do with it," Vicki finished C.J.'s train of thought. "We think that he might be in trouble."

CHAPTER 3

On the Case

"Hold it. We never said that he disappeared," the Captain said as he stuck his head out the door. "What makes you think that he has?"

"Simple," Vicki answered, "We just spent hours looking for him. And, he's not on any of the decks. It's like he's not on the ship."

"Sir, maybe we can help you find him," C.J. suggested.

"What can you girls do to help?" the Captain asked, regarding them suspiciously.

"Well, sir, we are detectives," Vicki replied.

"Detectives, you say? What are your names," the Captain asked.

"I'm Vicki Silver and this is C.J. Summers." Vicki answered, "You might not have heard of us, though. We're from Sport, Maine."

"Well, it's nice to meet you girls. I'm Captain Maguire and this is Jonathan Burns, one of the ship's stewards." Vicki looked closely at the older man. The Captain was in his early fifties with slightly gray hair. Jonathan wasn't much older than the girls. He was slightly taller than Joe, and had red hair and blue eyes.

"Can you tell us anything about this Steve Garcia," C.J. asked, "It could lead to a clue."

"Girls, I'm not at liberty to give out information about another passenger. Now, why don't you ladies return to your vacation and have a nice time on the ship. I'm sure these things will work themselves out."

"Well, thanks for your help, sir," C.J. said for both of them, "We'll be going now."

Once they were further down the hall," C.J. responded, "Right...Now let's go get Joe and Catlin and tell them what's going on."

They walked back towards their room, but stopped and knocked on Joe's door. Then they got Catlin from the next room. "Okay, what's going on?" Joe asked.

"Plenty," Vicki replied. She and C.J. clued them in, "It looks like we have a real case on our hands. We think we know who the strange man was."

Vicki continued, "Do you remember the announcement over the speaker shortly after we got on board. "They were paging a Mr. Steve Garcia to report to the Wedding Chapel."

Well, if I'm not mistaken, the man in the tuxedo was Mr. Garcia, and he was supposed to be getting married. But now he's missing. His bride must be frantic," Vicki said.

Vicki and C.J. watched as their friends thought about it.

"We're in," Joe said, "What can we do to help?"

"We need to search Mr. Garcia's room," Vicki replied, "...quietly. We don't want to alert the crew that we're investigating."

Joe and Catlin said, "No problem."

"Well, if you don't mind doing that for us, you would be doing us a big favor. If a crew member catches you, just do your best to explain without mentioning us."

"I'm in," Joe said, pounding a fist into his hand, "Come on Catlin, let's go search for clues. What's his room number?"

"It's number six hundred and one on the Aloha deck." Vicki told them, "Go before the Captain sends his security men to the room."

Joe and Catlin hurried to Mr. Garcia's room and slipped inside. "Okay," Joe said once they were in, "You search that side and I'll search this one." He walked over to the closet. He searched every pocket of every piece of clothing inside, and in one pocket he found a note.

"What's this," he asked himself. Picking it up, he read, 'Return the money by tonight, OR ELSE!' He stuck the note back in the pocket, careful to return it where he found it. "Did you find anything Catlin?"

"Yeah, I found a gym bag under the bed," Catlin answered. She pushed the gym clothes out of the way, and was surprised to discover something completely unexpected.

She stopped short and said, "Joe, come take a look at this." He came over and was also startled to see her discovery. The bottom of the bag was covered with bundles of money! There were stacks of hundred dollar bills 6" thick.

"This must be the money they were talking about," he said to himself.

"What?" Catlin asked, looking up at him.

"I found a note in a jacket telling him to come up with the money tonight. Maybe this is it," Joe said.

Catlin also found several pages from a financial ledger tucked in the side of the bag. As she began to examine the pages, suddenly there was a knocking on the door.

"Get out of there guys," came Vicki's voice, "Security is coming down." They closed the gym bag and put it back under the bed.

Catlin looked around quickly to make sure that everything was back in its proper place. Just then, Catlin spotted a piece of paper lying on top of the pillow. She picked it up and scanned it speedily.

Whatever she read was startling enough that her mouth dropped open and the paper started to shake in her hands. She silently read it again, but was pulled from her thoughts, as Joe called for her to hurry. She rushed out the door right behind Joe.

Joe and Catlin exited just before the security officers came down. The four teens went to Vicki and C.J.'s room.

"That was close," C.J. remarked, "Well, did you find anything?"

"We found a gym bag full of money," Joe said, "There were bundles of hundred dollar bills inside. I also found a note saying to bring the money tonight, or else."

"Did it say how much," Vicki asked.

"No, it didn't say," Joe replied, "But I would guess there's close to ten thousand dollars in that bag. I wonder what it was for."

"I wish we could ask him," Vicki said, "All we know is that Mr. Garcia had a lot of cash with him, and someone thinks he stole it."

"Vicki," Catlin said. "Do you think Mr. Garcia was upset enough to do something drastic?"

This got everyone's attention. Vicki looked at Catlin, and asked, "Catlin, why do you ask. What did you see?"

"It was a note. I found it on Mr. Garcia's pillow," Catlin trailed off, not wanting to continue.

Joe stepped in, "What did it say, Catlin? Go ahead, it's okay."

Catlin reluctantly continued, "Well, I don't remember it word for word, but it said something like, 'I'm ashamed of what I did, I embezzled a lot of money. I don't think Susan could forgive me. It would be easier if I go away.' Or, something like that."

Vicki said, "That sounds like a suicide note. Was it hand written?"

"No, it was typed. I think it was printed from a computer," Catlin said.

C.J. added, "We don't know what that means, and it could have been planted to throw off anyone investigating Mr. Garcia's disappearance."

"We have more questions about Mr. Garcia than answers at this point," Vicki said.

Joe chimed in to say, "Yeah, and we need to find him."

"We should try to find someone else on this ship who knows Mr. Garcia," C.J. interrupted, looking between them all, "We know there must be a bride onboard, and probably some family and friends who were going to attend the wedding. Let's start by asking the people staying in the rooms beside his."

As they walked into the hallway, they noticed a woman standing outside Mr. Garcia's room, talking with the security officers. "What do you mean he's missing?"

"We can't find him, Miss," a security officer told her, "We're still searching the ship for him." The woman suddenly became weak as her knees gave out beneath her. The officer held her up. "I'm sure we'll find him soon. Why don't you go to your room for now and let us do the searching? We'll let you know as soon as we find him." The woman nodded slowly and walked away. She could barely walk on her own.

"Let's go help her," Vicki said to C.J., "I think she knows him." She walked up to the lady and looked at her. She was slightly shorter than Vicki . She was very pretty with blonde hair and blue eyes. She looked to be in her late twenties.

The woman looked up as Vicki appeared beside her. "Yes, can I help you?" Vicki noticed that she was trying very hard not to cry.

"Actually, we were wondering if we could help you?" Vicki asked, "You look like you could use some help getting to your room."

"Yes, thank you," the woman replied, before hastily wiping at some un-fallen tears, "I must look like a mess." Vicki could tell that she was trying to control herself.

Vicki cautiously asked, "Do you mind if I ask how you know Mr. Garcia?"

"Oh, not at all. I'm Susan Morrow. Steve is my fiancé," Susan replied with query in her voice, as they began to proceed down the passageway. "Do you know Steve? Were you here for the wedding?"

"No, we don't really know Steve," Vicki responded. "I'm Vicki and this is my friend C.J. We believe we saw Steve earlier today on the Lido Deck. He seemed very stressed."

"How do you mean," asked Susan, in alarm, "Was he okay?"

"Well, he kept looking over his shoulder, as if someone was following him. Then he had an argument with another guy in the dance club."

"We wondered if that other man could have something to do with his disappearance?" C.J. added.

"I don't know," Susan replied, "He hasn't told me anything about a problem on the ship. I couldn't imagine what it could be." They then turned down the hallway.

Susan stopped and said, "This is my room here. Thank you girls for helping me...and for telling me what you know."

Vicki knew they hadn't actually revealed everything they knew. She wondered if Mr. Garcia would want Susan to see the ring Vicki was keeping in her pocket. It may have been a surprise that he wanted to reveal himself, at the wedding. And there was the note Catlin found on Steve's bed. It probably would not be a good idea to mention the suicide note to the bride, at least not until they were sure it was real.

Vicki said, "My cabin is on the same deck, number A seven-zero-seven. If you need anything, let us know. And, tell us if you hear anything more about your fiancé's disappearance."

"I guess I could. But how are you girls involved in all this," Susan asked, eyeing them curiously.

"Well, C.J. and I are detectives," Vicki said.

"You girls are detectives?" Susan questioned back and the girls affirmed this. Susan was silent as she thought for a moment. When Susan spoke again, she sounded slightly embarrassed, "I hope you don't think this is odd of me, but would you two be willing to investigate this for me? The security officers don't seem to be taking this very seriously. They don't know Steve like I do. He wouldn't just leave me standing at the altar, unless something was wrong."

Susan told them, "You know, Steve and I were supposed to get married before the ship departed today. Our families were here, and some of Steve's friends and co-workers, too. But,

Steve didn't show up at the chapel. Everyone who wasn't staying for the cruise had to get off before we could find out what happened to him."

Susan continued, "I know he wouldn't stand me up. Something must be wrong. I sure hope you girls are able to find him soon."

She continued, "I can't pay you much, but I could really use your help."

Vicki replied, "We would be glad to help."

There was a glimpse of hope in Susan's voice, as she said, "Do whatever you have to do to find Steve."

"We'll do our best," C.J. answered, "And, we'll be sure to let you know if we find anything more."

"I appreciate your help. And I'll tell you if I hear anything myself,"

Susan entered her room and locked it behind her.

"I hope we figure this out soon," Vicki said to C.J. They turned back to their friends and walked over. "We just had an interesting conversation," she told them, "As it turns out, that lady is Mr. Garcia's fiancée. They were supposed to get married before the ship departed today. I feel bad for her. It's her wedding day, and she can't find her groom."

"This must be awful for her," Catlin said, "And, she has no idea where Mr. Garcia disappeared to."

C.J. commented, "We have seven days to solve this mystery. We have to find him quickly, and hopefully unharmed."

"I agree," Joe said, "We need to figure out what's going on here and quick."

"The man we saw talking to Mr. Garcia is our obvious suspect, but we don't know who he is." Vicki said, "The real question is, why would somebody do this?"

Vicki was cut short when a scream rang throughout the deck!

CHAPTER 4

The Assailant

"That might have been Susan," Vicki yelled. She ran to Susan's room and tried the door. It was locked. "Susan, are you there!"

"Help," Vicki heard the woman scream.

Vicki stepped back and yelled, "Move back, I'm going to force open the door." Vicki aimed a kick and the door flew open. Vicki walked inside just as Susan raced out.

"Someone is in my room," Susan exclaimed, "He's still in there." Vicki walked into the room and looked around. She spotted a figure in the room, behind the curtains.

Vicki couldn't see his face. It appeared he was wearing a ski mask. She walked into the room to confront the man.

"Who are you?" Vicki asked as the man stepped out. He took a stance in front of Vicki and put his hands up for a fight. She rolled her eyes and looked at him, "I didn't come on a cruise to do this."

He threw a high punch but Vicki blocked it. He took a quick step backward, which allowed Vicki an opportunity. She pulled forward with a powerful punch that he narrowly avoided. He dodged to one side and got behind Vicki.

Suddenly, he grabbed one of Vicki's arms, but she quietly slipped her foot behind one of his and pulled. He staggered for a second and Vicki used the opening to punch him hard. He pulled back and raced out the door before anyone could stop him.

Susan again came face to face with the intruder as he rushed by. He darted down the passageway and around a corner.

"What's going on here?" one of the security men demanded as Vicki walked out.

"Sir," Susan explained in a frightened voice, "I found a man in my room. I couldn't see what he looked like, because he was wearing a mask. This young girl helped me, but the intruder got away. He went that way." She pointed down the passageway.

The officer asked, "Do you know why anyone would break into your room?"

"No," Susan answered, shaking her head, "I've got nothing of value in my room." She looked between Vicki and the officer, "Could it have something to do with my fiancé's disappearance?"

"It's too early to say ma'am," the officer replied, "Now, I'll need to take statements from both of you." He pulled out a pen and a small tablet.

"But you're letting him get away," Vicki argued, "Shouldn't you go after him?"

"Miss, I didn't see anyone come out of this room except you two ladies. I need a description of the man before I can start questioning anyone," he told her sternly. Just then Joe came on the scene.

Vicki bolted away from the room and headed down the passageway after the assailant. "Come back here," the officer yelled, "I need to ask you some questions." He moved to stop her, but Joe stepped in his way.

"It's okay," Joe said, "She can handle herself. I'm sure she would be glad to give you a statement later."

Vicki raced down the hallway, seeing the figure some distance in front of her. He was obviously the assailant. She saw him take a corner up ahead and was only seconds behind him.

She turned the corner and saw the man had stopped, waiting for her? Vicki didn't have time to react when he threw a powerful punch. She managed to step aside, but not far enough. She recoiled, stunned as the man made his escape. By the time she got back on her feet, he ran around the corner and disappeared into a crowd of passengers gathered at the elevators.

Vicki walked back to Susan's room, disappointed that she had lost the intruder. By then, security had left and her friends were waiting in the hall. "Did you catch him?" Catlin asked.

"No," Vicki answered, "He turned a corner and then ambushed me. While I was trying to get back up, he got away."

"Are you okay," Joe asked her.

"I'll be fine," Vicki replied, "I'd be even better if I had gotten him. He was fast, but I was close to nabbing him."

"The officer still needs to get a statement from you," Joe said, "He asked for you to see him at the security office near the bridge."

"I might as well go see him then," Vicki said, "I want to get it over with as soon as possible so I can get back to the case." She walked down the passageway, "I'll catch up with you guys later."

Vicki walked up to the ship's offices and knocked on the security office door. She heard someone call, "Come in." She stepped inside the small room.

The officer investigating the incident was sitting behind the desk. He motioned for her to sit. "Would you mind telling me why you ran off?" He stared her straight in the eyes.

"Not all at," Vicki replied, "I went after the assailant. I couldn't just let him get away after he tried to attack Susan." She stared back at him.

"Did you notice anything about this alleged assailant?" He asked, returning his eyes to the papers in front of him.

"He was broad-shouldered," Vicki replied, placing a hand to her mouth as she thought. "He walked kind of heavily, but he was fast. That's all I saw."

"Are you sure?" the officer asked.

"Positive," Vicki answered, "Why?"

"Oh, nothing," he said, "I still don't understand why you ran after him. As I understand it, you've never actually met Mr. Garcia. So why would you chase a dangerous man for someone you don't know?"

"My friends will tell you, I can't help it," Vicki replied, "I can't stand to see someone get away with a crime. Are you implying something?"

"Not at all," he answered, "I was just curious. It's just that most people would have let security handle a situation like that." Just then the door opened and Captain Maguire walked in.

"Someone told me I'd find you here," he said, turning to Vicki, "I told you that security would take care of this case. Young lady, you could be jeopardizing the investigation."

"Excuse me," Vicki protested, "I was walking by when Ms. Morrow cried out for help. I couldn't very well do nothing."

"I understand," he said, then folded his arms, "But before that you were seen talking with her in the hallway. How do you explain that?" Captain Maguire looked down at her.

"I saw that she was having trouble and I decided to help her," Vicki replied, "I would think you could understand. She could barely walk by herself. I offered to help her to her room." Vicki could tell that neither man was satisfied with her explanation. "Come on. My friends will vouch for me. Susan even asked us to investigate for her."

Captain Maguire looked at her harshly, "She doesn't have the authority to turn private detectives loose on my ship, to investigate a disappearance that may be nothing more than a groom with cold feet. I don't know everything that's going on here, but I want you to drop this case. This is serious and we don't need teenagers getting in the way."

He paused for effect, "Now ... I want you to go get your friends and meet me in my office in ten minutes." He turned and walked out the door before Vicki could respond.

Vicki turned to the officer, "Can I go now?" He nodded and she walked out. She walked downstairs to find Joe waiting by her door.

"So how did it go?" he asked.

"I had a run in with Captain Maguire," Vicki explained, "He told me to stay away from the case. But all he's done is make me want to solve it more."

"I know how it is," Joe said, "You hear this every time you try to investigate something. Adults don't want teenagers to handle something they think the police could handle better."

"And then we end up solving the case anyway," Vicki smiled, "Then the police have no choice but to thank us for helping to catch the criminal. That's the best part about being a detective."

Joe agreed, "They never know what to say when we solve the case. Chief Stevens even gave us an award for our last solved case."

Chief Stevens was in charge of the Police Force in Sport, Maine. Most of the cases they dealt with were in their own hometown, so they ran into Chief Stevens quite often.

"The Captain wants to meet with us," Vicki told Joe, remembering suddenly, "He didn't say why, but I don't think it is to congratulate our efforts thus far. Let's go round up C.J. and Catlin."

When the four met up in the Captain's office, he was sitting behind his desk, a piece of paper in front of him. It was the only object on the desk, so naturally their attention was drawn to it.

"There's a very good reason why I don't want you investigating this case," he began, standing to his feet, "and it is not just because I don't like the idea of teenagers messing up an investigation. You should know that in reality, there is no case."

"But he disappeared," Vicki exclaimed, both Joe and C.J. nodding in agreement. Catlin looked uncomfortable and scared. She eyed the paper curiously though she had an idea what it was. It was the same paper that she had seen on top of Steve's pillow and she knew exactly what it said.

"According to this," Captain Maguire held up one hand to quiet the group and with the other, gestured to the paper, "It is no mere accident that Steve Garcia went missing." Vicki and C.J. were immediately on their feet and leaned over the desk to read what it said. It appeared to be the note Catlin described finding in Mr. Garcia's room.

> TO WHOM IT MAY CONCERN,
>
> I, STEVE GARCIA, BEING OF SOUND MIND AND BODY, AND UNDER NO DURESS, WILLINGLY ADMIT THAT I AM SOLELY RESPONSIBLE FOR EMBEZZLING THE MISSING MONEY.
>
> YOU WILL FIND SOME OF THE MONEY IN MY ROOM, IN A GYM BAG. THIS IS ALL THE MONEY THAT IS LEFT.
>
> I AM TOTALLY ASHAMED OF WHAT I'VE DONE, AND I DON'T THINK SUSAN COULD EVER FORGIVE ME.
>
> IT WOULD BE EASIER FOR EVERYONE IF I WEREN'T AROUND ANY MORE.
>
> I'M SORRY, PLEASE FORGIVE ME,
> STEVE GARCIA

Neither of the girls let on that they knew of the note beforehand. After a few moments of reviewing the note, C.J. spoke up and queried, "Captain. Do you believe this is a suicide note, and that's why there is no case?"

"Well, certainly. That's clearly what it means," the Captain responded.

Vicki insisted, "Sir, with all due respect, the letter says Steve was guilty of embezzling from his own company. But, I specifically heard him say he wasn't responsible. Plus, he was supposed to get married today. Why would he jeopardize his new life with Susan by engaging in white collar crime?"

"Whether you believe it or not," Captain Maguire told them, walking around to the side of his desk, "this note, along with some other evidence we found in his room, proves that there is nothing more that we can do. All the evidence points to the fact that Steve Garcia didn't disappear...he jumped overboard."

Of course, Vicki knew the "other evidence" the Captain was speaking of, was the bag of money in Steve's room. But, in spite of everything the Captain said, she was still convinced, somehow, Steve was innocent of the charges, didn't write the note, and was still onboard.

The Captain concluded with, "I'm sorry to have to share this terrible news with you young people, but I thought you needed to know. You could ruin a perfectly good vacation on a wild goose chase. There's nothing more we can do for Mr. Garcia."

As the group was leaving the office, they were even more determined to find Mr. Garcia. "I think it's time we talk to Susan about the note," C.J. announced, "Maybe she can shed some light on it."

"It doesn't seem right," Joe jumped in, "Why would Steve jump overboard if he's supposed to be getting married?"

When they reached Susan's door a few minutes later, Susan answered the door with a box of tissue in hand. It was obvious the Captain had already told her about the note. She wiped her eyes hastily before stepping back to let them inside, "Did you hear about the note?"

"Yes, we just had a talk with Captain Maguire," C.J. began after the door was shut, "Susan, do you believe it's possible Steve jumped overboard."

"No, I don't believe a word of that note," Susan answered defiantly, "Steve's not the type. Besides, the note was prepared on a computer. There was no signature, or anything else to prove that Steve wrote it. I've been thinking it over and I'm standing by what I said. Steve is alive and he's somewhere on this ship."

Vicki said, "Susan. That's good enough for us. We'll continue to do what we can to find Mr. Garcia. By the way, do you have a photo of Steve we could use?"

Susan thought for a moment, and then reached for her purse. "I do have an engagement photo." She pulled it from her purse and reluctantly handed it to Vicki. "This is the photo we put in the paper to announce our wedding."

Vicki respectfully accepted it, and smiled at seeing the happy couple in the photo. "We'll take good care of it. It will be a big help as we talk to people on the ship about Steve's disappearance."

The group left Susan to herself, and went to formulate a plan.

CHAPTER 5

Captive

He had no idea where he was, but what little he could perceive with a blindfold over his eyes gave him a general idea. It felt cold and almost damp · "wherever he was". He could feel the hard floor on the backs of his arms where his skin met concrete.

Steve could not breathe very easily through the blindfold, but what he could inhale had a dank, musty odor.

Steve could taste was dried blood from a split lip. It was probably from the attack he could barely remember.

He recalled a knock and opening his cabin door. He had expected to see Susan or a member of his family, but instead he was greeted by a fist the second he opened the door. Now he felt foolish for not confirming who it was first. Maybe he wouldn't be in this situation if he had listened to instinct.

He had no idea where he was being held. It was obviously some rarely used storage room on the ship, as he could still feel the motion of the vessel. The only sound he could hear was the still silence of the stale air around him. The inviting warmth of the staterooms wasn't present.

Ropes bound his wrists and ankles. Steve felt fortunate they were bound in front instead of behind him.

The sudden noise of a key scraping into a lock drew his attention. The door creaked open and shut a moment later followed by heavy footsteps resounding off the walls.

A deep voice, which Steve knew sounded vaguely familiar, came as a person stood before him. "Here. Eat," the person said as a few slices of bread were pressed into Steve's hand, "I don't want you to starve now." The gravelly words were obviously muffled to disguise the captor's identity.

"Who are you?" Steve asked, his voice hoarse. But, he received no reply. After the attack, and barbaric treatment, he didn't expect anything else. Understandably, his captor would not want Steve to be able to identify him, but Steve continued the questions anyway, "Why are you doing this?"

"Eat your food," the man demanded, "I'm not coming back until tomorrow. You'll find out why soon enough."

Steve complied, as it was evident there was nothing else he could do.

After the man left, and Steve had enough food in his stomach to allow himself to think clearly again, his mind began to race. He desperately tried to piece together why he was in this predicament, and who he knew that would be capable of this kind of act.

Steve allowed himself to wonder back to the time when he and Susan met two years earlier.

A door chimed in a small Travel Agency in Portland, Maine. A businessman in his late twenties entered, putting away his umbrella after coming in from the rain. He had brown hair, and stood just over six-foot.

The two agents on duty each noticed as the man came in. Natasha was busy with another client, so Susan, the newest agent of the two, stood up and greeted the gentleman.

"Hello. Welcome to Crystal Seas Travel Agency," the young woman said. "How can I help you?"

Susan was in her mid twenties. Her long blonde hair had always gotten the attention of the guys, but usually the wrong type. She was captivated by the well-groomed gentleman that stood before her.

"I would like to book a cruise for next month. Do you have anything going to Quebec City in June," the businessman asked.

"Actually, we do have a six day cruise that departs on the twelfth. It will be coming in from Boston, and then continues on to Halifax,

Sidney, and then Quebec City. Here's a brochure," she said as she handed him the folded literature.

"Which ship will that cruise be on," the man asked.

"It's called the Crystal Waters," Susan replied.

"Does it have a wedding chapel," asked the man.

Susan was disappointed to hear the man mention a wedding, and immediately thought, 'well, there's another one off the market.'

But, she replied in a professional tone, "Actually, no sir. The only ship in our fleet with a wedding chapel is the Crystal Palace. It is our newest ship."

The man replied, "Well, we were determined to have the wedding as part of a cruise to Quebec City, so maybe you can tell me when the next time the Crystal Palace will be making that trip."

Susan went through the schedule, line by line, and stopped when she found the right combination of ship, schedule, and city stops. "Here it is," she said. "The Crystal Palace will be making a seven-day cruise starting on July the eighth. Do you think that will work for you and your fiancée," Susan asked.

"Actually, it's not for me. I'm trying to help a co-worker with some ideas for his wedding," the man said.

Susan, looked at the man again, with new interest. "Well, in that case," she said, "Here's a different brochure for the Crystal Palace, and a schedule for the July eighth cruise."

Susan continued, "I'm Susan Morrow, by the way."

"Steven Garcia," the man replied. He shook her delicate hand gently, and said, "But, you can call me Steve."

CHAPTER 6

The Hunt

"Want to go look around the dance club again?" Vicki asked first thing in the morning, "Maybe someone has seen Mr. Garcia."

"That's sounds good," Joe replied, "Let's head there now." Together, they walked up to the dance club. The room was still packed with teenagers, like it had been the previous day, and they were lucky to find seats in the back. "Who should we ask?" He glanced around at all the unfamiliar faces.

"Her," Vicki answered, pointing to the waitress heading their way. Joe recognized her as Simone, the same woman who had served them the day before.

"What can I get you?" the waitress asked as she approached.

"Nothing at the moment. But could you tell us something?" Vicki asked. She waited for the approving nod. "Have you seen the man in this picture come in here recently? He was last seen wearing a tuxedo." The girl thought a moment before answering, "Nope, sorry. It's hard to remember everyone who comes in here all day. Why, is it important?"

"It could be. He's missing." Vicki said, "Look. Maybe someone else who works here saw him recently."

"Are you sure he came in here?" the waitress asked. "I'll show this to the maitre d'. I'll be right back." Vicki and Joe were silent while waiting for her to come back. "Yes," the girl said when she returned, handing the photo back to Vicki, "The maitre d' said that he believes he saw this man yesterday. Would you like to talk to him?"

"Yes," Vicki said, "Thank you." Vicki and Joe walked to the front of the club. "Excuse me," she asked the man. He looked at her, "I was asking about that man you may have seen yesterday."

"Yes, I'm Brian," the man replied, "What do you want to know?" Brian was six feet tall with black hair and light blue eyes.

"Was he alone," Vicki asked, immediately getting to the point.

"No," Brian thought for a moment, "I saw him talking to another man in that booth over there." Brian gestured in the direction of the booth Vicki had seen Steve in the day before. "They talked for a few minutes and then he left. He seemed upset. If I recall correctly, the man ran into some other passengers on the way out." Vicki and Joe looked at each other and tried to hide their disappointed smiles. They were the young couple the man was talking about.

"Did you notice anything strange?" Joe cut in, "Did he do anything out of the ordinary?"

"Well," Brian thought, "He looked really upset, like something was bothering him."

"Do you happen to know the man he was speaking with?" Joe asked.

"No," Brian replied, "He never turned in my direction and I didn't stop to think about it at the time."

"Well, thanks," Vicki said, trying not to sound too discouraged, "You've been very helpful. Do you have any idea where he went after that?"

"Yes, he walked towards the stairs. I assume he went to a lower deck." Vicki and Joe thanked him and quickly left the club. They turned and went back down the stairs.

Vicki walked to the room that she and C.J. shared. She realized that the door was hanging slightly open. "C.J.," she called out, "Are you in there?" There was no answer. She opened the door and took a step back. The room had been destroyed!

CHAPTER 7

The Evidence

Vicki cautiously walked into the room in order to see the damage more clearly. The dresser drawers had been pulled out and hangers from the closet lay on the floor. The dresser top had been completely cleared off, the contents strewn about.

Soon C.J. came up, "Vicki," she called upon entering, then stopped in her tracks at the scene, "What happened?"

"Our room's been ransacked," Vicki told her.

"But, who did this?" C.J. asked, "I was only gone for ten minutes."

"I found the door open," Vicki explained, "They must have gotten inside pretty easily. These staterooms don't have the best locks, and it probably didn't take long to ransack a room this size."

The girls took a look around. They picked up all their stuff and put it back where it belonged. Throughout their search, it appeared nothing was missing.

"This doesn't appear to have been a robbery if you ask me." C.J. remarked, "They didn't even touch my money. I found it on the floor." She held up a small stack of folded dollar bills.

"Everything's here," Vicki agreed, "I wonder who did this and what they were looking for?"

"Maybe we should report this to security," C.J. suggested.

"No, we don't need to report this. Nothing was taken and everything's fine otherwise. Besides, the security guards probably wouldn't be too happy to see us anyway."

"Alright. I guess you have a point," C.J. agreed, "But, we will need to be more careful. Obviously, whoever is involved with the disappearance of Mr. Garcia, has found out where our room is."

"C.J., let's try to figure out who our suspects are," Vicki suggested.

"You know. I hate to say it, but Susan could be a suspect," C.J. admitted after a few moments, "We did tell her where our room was." She paused, and then continued, "The only other person who would know would be the captain."

"You must be kidding," Vicki shook her head, "Susan's engaged to Steve, and the Captain would have no motive."

"Look at it this way," C.J. replied, "Susan is marrying this rich guy. So, if something were to happen to him, who would get his money? He would leave it to her, right?"

"We don't know that," Vicki said with a sigh, "Besides, what could she gain by kidnapping him before the wedding? A spouse might be awarded insurance money if her husband disappeared, but a fiancée wouldn't. And, unless she can act, what happened yesterday seemed real enough to me. Did you see how upset she was?"

"I noticed," C.J. responded, "But think about it. How could you not notice a strange man in your room?"

"I don't know," Vicki replied, "Maybe he hid so she wouldn't see him. I know it doesn't look good, but I don't think she's behind it."

"We have to cover every angle, though," C.J. said, "I'm not saying that she did it, only that it's possible."

Vicki finally agreed, "Okay, who else?"

"What about the man Steve spoke to in the Dance Club, and the man who hid in Susan's room?" C.J. asked.

Vicki replied, "They could be the same person. The only problem is, we don't know who either one of them is."

"I'll go check up on Susan," Vicki finally decided, "I'm sure she'll talk to me about this." She walked out the door and turned in the direction of Susan's room. She knocked quietly.

"Come in," Susan called. Vicki entered, "Hi, Vicki. Do you have any news?"

"I came to see how you were doing," Vicki replied, "Would you mind if I looked around for any clues? You just never know what might lead to something."

"Go right ahead, if that will help," Susan said, allowing Vicki to pass her. She looked at Vicki anxiously, "Do you know anything more since yesterday?"

"Some," Vicki said, "The maitre d' at the Dance Club confirmed what I saw yesterday. He saw Steve talking to a man at the table."

Vicki became distracted with a glinting object on the floor, just under the edge of the bed. She knelt on the ground. Grabbing a tissue, she picked up the mysterious item, "Did you lose a pocketknife?"

"No," Susan replied, shaking her head, "I don't even own one."

"Does Steve have a pocketknife?" Vicki again queried.

Susan replied, "No. Not that I am aware of."

"Well, then somebody else must have dropped this," Vicki said as she continued to look for anything out of the ordinary.

"Well, I don't see anything else. If you don't mind, I'll take this pocketknife with me and use it in our investigation." Susan nodded her approval, and Vicki returned to her room.

"Hey, C.J," she said, "Look what I found in Susan's room. The intruder must have dropped it." Vicki showed her friend the pocketknife. C.J. picked it up in the tissue, and examined it closely.

"This is great Vicki," C.J. replied, "Maybe we'll be able to get prints off of it."

"Yeah, but how?" Vicki asked, "We don't exactly have the equipment to do that."

C.J. smiled slyly, and said, "I bet we can put together a fingerprint kit with just the things in this room."

C.J. scanned the room, and gathered four objects, which included a finger nail file, a piece of paper, a pencil, and some cellophane tape.

First, she ripped the paper in two, and folded one of them in half. Then, she took the pencil and ground off some of the lead with the finger nail file into the center of the folded paper. Next, she carefully poured the lead filings over the knife, tamping off any excess.

The last step in the process was to pick up the prints off the knife with the tape. She then laid the tape down onto the half sheet of paper. After lifting as many prints as she could from all surfaces of the knife, she handed the sheet to Vicki.

"What do you think, Vicki?" C.J. asked with pride.

Vicki replied, "That's pretty cool, C.J. Who knew you could make a fingerprint kit out of the stuff in our room. And the prints are fairly clear, too."

C.J. asked, "Do you think they are good enough to take to the security office?"

"I'm sure they are, C.J.," Vicki said, "But if Captain Maguire finds out we've been investigating the case, he'll get even angrier with us. He's already warned us twice to lay off."

"What else can we do?" C.J. asked, "We don't have any prints to compare them with."

"Let's just hang onto them until we do have some other prints to compare them with." She put the knife and prints into a plastic bag and set them aside.

Afterwards, Vicki walked back up to the third floor, where she hoped to look for more clues. Shortly, she found Joe at one of the restaurants and joined him. She told him about what they had found. "We don't know where to look next," Vicki concluded, "We only have two suspects. The one doesn't have a motive, and the other doesn't have a name."

"Is Susan one of your suspects?" asked Joe.

Vicki replied, "I hate to say it, but yes. How did you know?"

"You always go for the least likely suspect," Joe said with a smile.

Joe continued, "If Susan is one of your suspects, don't you think you should go through her room more thoroughly?"

"You're right," Vicki said. "But we would need her out of the room for a while."

"Well," Joe replied, "We could just ask her to step out for a while, and tell her we need to search her room more thoroughly."

Vicki said, "I would like to, Joe. But, you never know what a suspect might conceal, even subconsciously."

Joe replied, "I understand. I could invite her for a walk. She probably needs to get out and about for a while. Just be sure you are careful with her things. We don't want to damage anything. And remember, we are only doing this so we can find Steve."

"Okay," Vicki consented, "Just keep her out for about 15 minutes. That should give me enough time." She and Joe walked down to Susan's room. Vicki watched from around the corner as he knocked on her door.

"Hello. This is Joe ... um ... Vicki's boyfriend. I was wondering if you would like to walk around the ship a few minutes," he asked the woman, "It might be good for you to get some fresh air."

She opened the door about halfway, and said, "I don't know. I really should stay here in case they find out something about Steve."

"Don't worry, we will only be gone a few minutes," Joe reassured her.

"Alright," Susan reluctantly agreed with a sigh, "I'll go. Maybe you're right, it could be good for me." The two walked out and up to the next floor. Once they were out of sight, Vicki entered Susan's room. Suddenly a voice called, "Wait a minute. I forgot my bag."

"You won't need it," Vicki heard Joe say, "We'll be right back."

"Okay, if you say so," Susan replied hesitantly. Vicki felt relieved when their voices faded away.

Vicki turned back to the room. It was growing dark. Vicki spotted Susan's purse on the bed and picked it up, careful to put on some gloves first.

In the light of her flashlight, Vicki could see that inside the purse was some makeup, including lipstick, blush, eyeliner, and eye shadow. Also inside was a bottle of perfume. She pushed those items aside and looked beneath them. She found a folded piece of paper at the bottom! Lifting it out of the purse, she hesitated before opening it. Knowing she had to fully investigate Steve's disappearance, she decided to open it.

The note read,

My Darling Susan,

I made all the arrangements today for the cruise.

I'm so excited about the wedding, and it will be great to spend time with you on the ship.

A cruise is just what we need after the wedding.

I can't wait until we can start our lives together in our new home.

May God grant us a lifetime of happy memories as we start our new family.

Love forever,

Steve

Vicki was touched by the sentiment, and she too prayed that God would bring Steve and

Susan back together so they could begin their lives together, the way it was intended.

Vicki placed the note back in the purse and looked some more. In the side pocket, she found more notes. One in particular caught her attention. It had several small water stains, presumably from Susan's tears.

She opened it, and scanned the page.

The note read,

Susan,

I'm sorry that it happened like this, but something is very wrong right now.

Once I am able to figure this out, I'll try to explain. But, for now, I want you to be safe. Which means I need to take care of this on my own. I'll contact you when I can.

Again, I am really sorry, but this is for the best. I wouldn't want anything to happen to you.

Please, don't be upset. I need you to be strong so we can get through this.

Love Forever,

Steve

"Interesting," Vicki spoke aloud to herself, "Why didn't Susan tell me about this note?"

Vicki thought to herself, 'All of the notes were handwritten, which seems to agree with Susan's claim that Steve wouldn't type a personal note. It seemed that Steve was a bit sentimental.'

Vicki replaced the notes in the purse and turned to the dresser. On the very top was a small box. It was dark blue in color and was made of velvet. She carefully picked it up and opened it. Just like the other box Vicki had, this one also contained a ring, only this one was golden with a large diamond in the middle. And, circling the diamond were several blue gems.

Vicki said to herself, "This must be Susan's engagement ring. "Why isn't she wearing it though," Vicki wondered. She looked back on the dresser. Another box was lying on top. Thinking it was more jewelry, Vicki picked it up. Instead of jewelry though, there was a small message inside. It read "I know where Steve is. Watch your back or the same thing could happen to you."

Vicki closed both boxes and took a cautious step back. She looked around the room for a sign that anyone else was there. Suddenly, the door began to slowly creak open.

Vicki shut off her flashlight, took a step back and ducked into the closet. She hid just as the door fully opened. A dark figure walked inside. A flashlight beam shown across the room.

Vicki held her breath as the light swept in her direction! She prayed that she wouldn't be spotted!

CHAPTER 8

The Chapel

As Joe and Susan walked down the corridors, Joe could sense that Susan was deeply troubled by all the events of the day.

"Susan", Joe said, "how about we take a walk along the Sun Deck. You can take in the ocean for a while."

Susan replied, "If you don't mind, I'd rather not. If Steve really did go overboard, the last thing I want to see right now is the ocean."

Joe nodded his understanding.

Susan continued in her thoughts, when she began to wonder in a quiet voice, "I wish we had never decided to mix Steve's business with our wedding plans. He thought it would be a way to save money, and time, but now I think it's why he's missing."

Joe queried, "You think Steve's business is responsible for his disappearance? Why do you think that?"

Susan looked around, and seemed concerned that Joe was asking questions out loud. "Please, I don't want to say too much out here in the open. All I can say is, Steve was going to meet up with some of his business associates here on the ship tomorrow."

Susan," Joe asked quietly, "If you know any of the names of Steve's associates, it could be a big help in finding him."

"I haven't actually met anyone at his office, but Steve has spoken about a man by the name of Bill Dobbs. I think he who works for Steve in the accounting department. He's here, along with Steve's boss, Mark Chapman."

Susan continued, "And, based on the note, someone wants us to believe Steve is responsible for a bunch of missing money."

Joe replied, "I see."

"But, let's not talk about that now." Susan asked, "Would you mind if we went by the chapel. I would like to talk to Chaplain Nahalea."

"Sure, Susan. No problem," Joe said, "That sounds like a good idea."

After a few minutes of walking corridors and the elevator ride to the Promenade Deck, they arrived at the Wedding Chapel. It was an elegantly appointed room that seated about fifty people. It was lined with beautiful wood paneling and inlaid accents. Stained glass windows adorned each side of the altar, which held a golden cross.

There were several stewards in the room removing white lace decorations from the pews.

The candleholders were being boxed up, and several flower decorations were being placed in bags to be used for some future wedding.

On seeing the activities, Susan stopped in the door and dropped her gaze to the floor. She reached for Joe's arm and sobbed. It was too much for a bride to see her wedding taken apart before it even happened.

Joe did what he could to comfort the young woman, but felt inadequate to understand what she must be going through.

"Susan," Joe asked, "are you sure you want to do this?"

Just then, a voice called from the other side of the room. "Susan, you shouldn't be seeing this." The chaplain hurried from across the room, and led Susan into the corridor.

"Dear, Susan. I was so sorry to hear that Steve is missing. When he didn't show at the wedding this morning, I knew something must have been wrong," the Chaplain said, and then paused. "Because, that young man was determined to marry you today."

Lifting Susan's chin, the Chaplain said with a smile, "And God willing, he will marry you soon. And all of this will be put back together, just the way you wanted it. We'll have a great ceremony, and your lives together will begin just the way you dreamed."

Susan strained a smile, in appreciation for the Chaplain's kind words.

"And who is this young man?" The Chaplain asked.

"Hello, sir. I'm Joe Clark. My friends and I were here for the cruise, when we learned about Mr. Garcia's disappearance on the ship. We've been trying help Susan find him," Joe said.

Chaplain Nahalea said, "Well, that is very kind of you and your friends. Susan can use all the help she can find right now. I'm sure with the Lord's help, you'll find Mr. Garcia soon."

"Joe," Susan explained, "Chaplain Nahalea is from Kauai, Hawaii, and is a friend of Steve.

"Yes, that's right," agreed the chaplain, "Cousin Steve and I have known each other for some time. Now that is a man who has been praying for a wife, and look who God brought him," Chaplain Nahalea smiled at Susan, hoping to cheer her up.

"Cousin?" asked Joe.

"Yes," the chaplain confirmed, "In Hawaii, we call everyone cousin. It's our way of making everyone feel like family."

"But, my real concern, is Cousin Susan," the chaplain said as he turned to Susan, "Have you learned anything new? Does anyone have any ideas where Steve may have gone?"

Susan spoke softly, as if not wanting to hear her own words, "They found a note in Steve's room." Susan stopped, choking back the emotions, "It was horrible. Someone planted a note in his room, to make it look like he wanted to end his own life. The note claimed he embezzled money from his own company. I know he didn't write that note, and I know he wouldn't do something dishonest."

The Chaplain at first looked shocked. After a moment his countenance changed to one of resolve. "Susan, I agree. There is no way Steve would do something like that."

He continued, "You know, Steve shared with me his faith, and his belief in a loving God. And anyone who knows God, knows there is nothing they can do to earn God's love. And also, there is nothing they can do that God won't forgive."

The Bible says in First John chapter one and verse nine, 'If we confess our sins, He is faithful and just to forgive us our sins, and to cleanse us from all unrighteousness.'

"Now, I believe Steve has a personal relationship with Jesus. And, I don't believe he would purposely do anything to bring shame on himself or you. But even if he did, and the Lord knows that none of us are perfect, Steve knows he has a loving Father that would forgive him."

He looked intently in Susan's eyes, and said, "And Steve knows that you would forgive him, too. So, there's absolutely no reason Steve would do such a thing. Rest assured in that."

Chaplain Nahalea continued, "I'm sure he's doing what he can to resolve this situation, clear his good name, and get back here so you two can get married."

"Thank you," Susan said with some encouragement in her voice. "Thank you for reminding me what I already knew. I'm sure Steve will be back soon."

"And I'm praying God will protect him, and keep him safe, until he can return," the Chaplain concluded.

"Thank you for your prayers. You are such a blessing." Susan turned to Joe, "I think it's time we head back, and see if there is any news."

"Okay," Joe said. He extended his hand to Chaplain Nahalea, "Sir, it was great to meet you. I feel like you've encouraged us both. I've always known there was a loving God, and that I can have a personal relationship with Him. But, it is great to see how His Word can be applied in even the toughest situations."

"Come back anytime, Cousin Joe. And thank you for helping Susan during this time," Chaplain Nahalea said.

"Yes, sir," Joe said as he began to lead Susan back towards her room.

CHAPTER 9

Dark Hours

Steve wondered how long it had been since he had been thrown into the room. He could feel the metal of his watch against his skin, but couldn't see what time it was because of the blindfold and restraints.

Surely, by now, someone would be looking for him. Would Susan enlist the help of the ship to find him? Perhaps he would be found eventually, but a tiny doubt lay in the back of Steve's mind.

Steve's first thoughts were about Susan. He hoped she wouldn't worry too much, but he knew she would. That was something absolutely certain about this situation.

He had tried to prepare her for the rough road ahead with the note, but now he wondered if it would keep her from notifying the authorities of his disappearance.

If he had known there would be danger on the cruise, he never would have suggested it in the first place. At the time, it seemed like a good idea. Hold the annual business meeting on a cruise ship, that way the office can pay for it. And, he and Susan could get married and have a honeymoon at the same time.

Either way, Steve knew that something was terribly wrong if someone was willing to kidnap an officer of the company. When the president of AGM, Allied Global Merchandising, approached him about the money, accusing him of embezzlement, warning bells immediately went off in his mind.

Until he found out for sure, Steve had only his few suspicions, and a lot of questions, to keep him company in the dark hours.

Again, Steve allowed himself to reflect on those early days of his and Susan's relationship. About six months earlier, Steve finally got the nerve to propose to Susan.

The two had been dating for well over a year. They both knew that something special was happening, and their bond grew day by day.

For Steve and Susan, it wasn't a matter of if Steve would propose, but when. Susan was patient, and would wait for Steve to find the right time.

From the beginning of their relationship, Susan made it clear, that theirs would have to be a unique courtship. She believed in purity until marriage – to the point that the two agreed not to so much as kiss until their wedding day.

Shortly before meeting Susan, Steve had rededicated himself to God. He wanted God to bring the right person into his life, and he found Susan to be that special one.

Before Susan, Steve had various relationships with young women, and was not satisfied. He knew it was not God's best for him. He was glad to finally meet a woman who was so dedicated to the Lord, that she would focus more on getting to know the man, than in a romantic adventure that would only lead to disappointment.

The time came for Steve to propose. He knew to wait any longer would only frustrate them both, and would delay the blessings God had for them.

He first went to Susan's parents, who had come to know him well over time, and they were happy to relay their blessings. He next went to his pastor, who agreed, after coming to know Susan, that God had brought the two of them together.

Steve decided on the place and time, and then put his plan into action.

Susan was busy at work, taking calls and helping customers. A small crowd began to gather in front of the windows at the small travel agency. At first, no one noticed, since so many people tended to gather at that corner. But, eventually, as the room grew dark from all the silhouetted figures, Natasha and Susan began to wonder what the commotion was.

Susan was shocked when she began to recognize the figures in the window as her friends, Steve's co-workers, her parents, and Steve's pastor.

She started for the door when a text message came over her phone. It read, 'SM+SG+G=4E'. And, it was from Steve.

Just then, Steve walked through the door, with a bouquet of flowers in hand, and walked to Susan's desk.

He began, "Susan, I know this day has been a long time coming. I thought of all the places I could ask you this question. I could have selected our favorite restaurant and given you my proposal in alphabet soup. Or, we could have gone to a ball game, and seen my proposal on the jumbo-tron. I could have taken you to the park, and hired a plane to write a message in the sky. But, I wanted to do this at the place we first met, with the people who care about us, here to witness my most important question."

Steve pulled a small box from his pocket. It was covered in dark blue velvet. And, from it he pulled a ring. It was gold with a large diamond in the middle, which was encircled with blue gems. Inside the band was the inscription 'SM+SG+G=4E'.

Finally, Steve posed the question he had been waiting to ask for so long, "I believe that Susan Morrow plus Steven Garcia plus God equals forever. Will you marry me?"

The crowd didn't wait for her response, which came amid cheers and howls, as she said, "I will".

That was six months ago. Here it was, time for their wedding, and somehow they were separated. Steve did not question God's purpose, he only wondered about God's timing.

All of their hopes and dreams rested on starting their lives together as husband and wife, with God's blessings. He believed it was just a matter of when.

CHAPTER 10

Door to Door

Vicki watched as the light barely scanned past the place where she was hiding. She opened the door a slit and peered out, hoping she wouldn't draw any attention to herself in the process. The figure was moving around the room, looking for something.

She saw him move closer to the closet where she was hiding. When the intruder was close enough, she swung the door open, knocking him down.

"Hold it," the person called in a familiar voice, "It's me."

"C.J.," Vicki exclaimed, opening the door and rushing out, "What are you doing here?" She walked over and helped her to her feet.

"Sorry," C.J. replied, "I wanted to help you look around for clues."

"Thanks for scaring me," Vicki told her, "but I've already found several clues. We should get out of here before Susan and Joe come back. I'm sorry for hitting you like that."

"I'm okay," C.J. told her, "I didn't even see you until you slammed the door into me."

"Sorry," Vicki said again, "But at least you said something before I could do any more damage."

C.J. stood up and left with Vicki right behind her. Vicki locked the door and both girls headed off.

Vicki unlocked the door to their room and entered. C.J. went and sat on her bed. "Okay. What did you find?" she asked her friend.

Vicki told her about the engagement ring and repeated the contents of the two notes as best she could remember.

"So it looks as if Susan knows more than she's letting on," C.J. said after Vicki was done, "Why didn't she tell us about these things? That definitely puts the case in a new perspective."

"Maybe she's afraid that if she revealed everything she knows, something might happen to her or Steve." Vicki remarked, "Mr. Garcia said in one of the notes that he was worried about her safety. Maybe she thought something might happen to him, so she kept quiet."

"Makes sense," C.J. agreed, "but I wish she would tell us what she knows. It sounds like a lead. She knows something is going on, but she doesn't know exactly what it is. It isn't much, but it's a start. What do you think we should do next?"

"We need more suspects," Vicki said, "The only two we have don't seem to fit the part. They don't have a good enough motive. We need to ask around some more."

C.J. agreed, "Somebody on this ship, besides Susan, knows Steve," and with that, the two girls headed out.

"Vicki," Joe called out, "I have something that you might want to hear." Vicki and C.J. waited for Joe to catch up.

"You're back. I take it Susan has returned to her room," asked Vicki.

"Yes, I dropped her off just a moment ago," Joe said.

"We were about to look for some family or friends of Steve," C.J. said. "Was there something you wanted to say?"

"Yes, when I was talking to Susan, she said several of Steve's business associates are onboard. A man by the name of Bill Dobbs works for Steve in the accounting department. And Steve's boss is here, too. His name is Mark Chapman."

"You see," said Joe. "They weren't just here to get married. Steve's company was going to have their annual business meeting onboard, tomorrow."

"So all we have to do is find one of Steve's business associates," C.J. asked, "Does Susan know what Bill Dobbs or Mark Chapman looks like?"

"No," Joe replied, "She hadn't actually spoken to anyone at Steve's office before. We could try to get ahold of the reservation book and see where their rooms are."

"But how are we going to do that," Vicki asked, "We can't just walk into the Purser's Office and ask to see the list. Captain Maguire is already angry at us."

"We'll just have to do some more sneaking around," C.J. stated, "I don't see any other way. Do you think you can handle it?"

"You bet I can," Vicki told her with a grin, "We just need to make sure there's no one around." The three teenagers walked out and headed for the upper deck. They quickly found their way to the Purser's Office. Vicki made sure to knock before entering.

Luckily, the door was unlocked and nobody was inside. She easily found the logbook and scanned the list until she found the names Bill Dobbs and Mark Chapman. She looked across the sheet and saw that Mr. Dobbs was in room B three-zero-three on the Baja Deck, and Chapman was in room B three-zero-four. Once Vicki had acquired the information they needed, she quickly exited the room.

"Okay, I got the room numbers," she said and told her friends, "Now let's go see how Steve's business associates are connected." They walked down to room B three-zero-three and knocked quietly. There was an immediate answer.

"Go away," the man yelled through the closed door, "I don't need anything right now."

"Mr. Dobbs," C.J. called, "We understand that you are an associate of Mr. Garcia's."

"I think you two can handle this," Vicki whispered, "I'm going to ask Susan a few questions." Vicki turned and ran down the hallway. Mr. Dobbs' door suddenly flew open a moment later.

"I was," Mr. Dobbs answered. A man slightly taller than Vicki opened the door. His brown hair was slicked back and his green eyes studied them silently. He looked to be around thirty. "So what. What do you kids want?"

"We were just wondering if you would answer some questions," Joe replied.

"Not that it's any of your business," Bill Dobbs answered, "but Garcia was supposed to join us for a business meeting tomorrow, but now that he's disappeared, that seems unlikely. And, I'm stuck on this horrid ship." Before the two could do anything, he slammed the door in their faces.

"He was helpful," C.J. stated sarcastically.

"Mr. Dobbs," Joe called again, "We didn't get to ask all of our questions." There was no answer from inside. "I guess he doesn't want to talk to us." Joe knocked louder.

"Let's try again later," C.J. suggested, putting a hand on his arm as a signal to stop knocking, "We don't need to draw a lot of attention to ourselves right now. Let's try Mr. Chapman's room on the other side."

The two walked across the deck, to room B three-zero-four, and again knocked. This time there was no answer. Having decided not to break into the stranger's room, the two went looking for Vicki.

At that moment, Vicki was sitting in Susan's room, "Susan," she said slowly, "I think you know more than you're letting on."

"I don't know anything," Susan answered abruptly, "This whole thing is a mystery to me. I don't know who would do any of this...or why." Vicki knew there were several things that Susan was trying to conceal.

"Susan, if you know anything about this, you should say something," Vicki said, "It could save your fiancé's life if you tell us what you know."

"I already told you, I don't know anything," the woman said, "I don't know, I just don't."

"Okay," Vicki held up her hands, "I know when to give up. If you don't want to tell us anything, I can't do anything about it. I just thought you would want to do everything possible to make sure Steve was found safe." Vicki stood up and turned towards the door. She had her hand on the doorknob before she was halted.

"Okay, okay. Maybe there is something," Susan said reluctantly, "But it's not much. This morning I found a letter from Steve saying something was wrong, and he was concerned for my safety. I knew he must be in some trouble. And whatever it was, it was so bad that he couldn't tell me what it was about."

"Anything else," Vicki asked.

"Well," Susan paused. "Yes ... when I saw him at the wedding rehearsal last night, he was acting so nervous. He was called away in the middle of our rehearsal dinner. He left in a terrible hurry. And besides that, someone followed him out the restaurant. I wonder now if it had something to do with this." Susan looked up at Vicki, "Do you think there is any chance we will find him...alive?"

"Susan, we're doing everything we can. Don't lose hope. Listen, Joe went to check out the business associates you told him about...Mr. Dobbs and Mr. Chapman. I think there's a chance one of them might have been threatening Steve. That's all we know right now. But, we'll keep looking." Vicki walked out and immediately ran into C.J. and Joe. "Did you find anything?"

"No," C.J. answered, "Mr. Dobbs slammed the door in our faces. We couldn't get him to talk to us after that. And, Mr. Chapman didn't answer his door, or wasn't in his room. How did you do?"

"Susan finally admitted to receiving the note from Steve about being in trouble," Vicki said, "I think she believes Steve's disappearance has something to do with his business. I wish there was more we could do."

"I know," C.J. said, "We'll keep trying to talk to Mr. Dobbs and Mr. Chapman. According to Mr. Dobbs, they were supposed to have a business meeting tomorrow. That was all we got out of him. When we mentioned that we wanted to ask him some more questions, he just got angrier. We'll give him some time to cool down before we try again."

"That's probably a good idea," Joe said, "I don't think he'll want to see us for a while." Just then everyone turned as a woman in her twenties approached and knocked on Steve Garcia's door. She was about five foot four with brown hair.

"Steve," she called, "We need to talk." Vicki and the others knew she wouldn't get an answer.

"Excuse me," Vicki called out to her, "Mr. Garcia is not in right now." The woman turned to glare at the three. Her brown eyes narrowed upon seeing them.

"What do you mean he's not in," she demanded, "I need to speak with him now! He owes me an explanation."

"What did he do," C.J. asked.

"He was supposed to meet me this morning," she answered angrily, "He put my company in a huge bind. We were supposed to discuss a business deal, but he didn't show. I've been trying to find him for hours."

"I'm sorry to hear that," Vicki said and introduced herself and her friends, "If we see him, who should we say wants to talk to him?"

"Tell him that Angela Hensen needs to talk to him right away, I'm in room A five-twenty-six on this deck," Angela turned and huffed off. Then she turned back, "And he had better call me. He owes my company a rather large explanation."

"That was interesting," Vicki said, as she walked out of sight, "I'd say she has as much reason to find Mr. Garcia as anyone."

"We have a very interesting suspect list," C.J. remarked, "Some have motive to put Mr.

Garcia out of the picture, and others want to find him as quickly as possible."

"With this last bit of information," Vicki stated, "I think the picture is starting to come together. I suggest we each take a suspect and see what we can find out."

"I'll take Angela," C.J. said, "There may be more she wants to say."

"If it's okay with you, Vicki," Joe asked, "I'll continue to work with Susan."

"That's fine," Vicki said, "I'll take on Mr. Dobbs. He hasn't met me yet, so maybe he'll let something slip." She smiled confidently, "He won't know what hit him. "

"And," Vicki continued, "I'll ask Catlin to speak with Jonathan – the steward. Since he works directly with the Captain, and the security staff, he might know something that could help."

The three separated and left to check out their suspects.

CHAPTER 11

Suspect Number One

After telling Catlin her assignment, Vicki walked down the hallway towards Bill Dobbs' room, determined to get answers. She came up to the door and knocked. "What do you want," asked a gruff voice on the other side.

"Mr. Dobbs, my name is Vicki Silver. I'm investigating the disappearance of Mr. Garcia."

Dobbs popped the door open, "Like I told your friends, beat it."

"Mr. Dobbs, please," Vicki pleaded, "You need to hear this."

Mr. Dobbs stood defiantly at the door, "What? What's so important?"

Vicki pushed through, "Mr. Garcia has disappeared, and no one has seen him since this morning."

Mr. Dobbs replied gruffly, "Tell someone who cares."

"I thought I was," Vicki answered, "Don't you care what's happened to your boss? He missed his own wedding, and on a ship that's out to sea. Something is wrong!"

Mr. Dobbs took a step back. He obviously wasn't used to being talked to in such a forceful manner. Vicki hoped that she had hit a soft spot.

He turned to her angrily, "Yeah, I understand. So, he disappeared? That's too bad!" He tried to close the door again, but Vicki walked in.

"Get out!" he demanded.

"Not until I get some answers," Vicki replied evenly, "Your boss may have been accused of a crime, and threatened. If you know anything about it, you need to come forward."

"What's worse, is Steve had reason to be concerned for his fiancée's safety. He warned her that something was going on, and she could be in danger. He disappears, and then someone broke into his fiancée's room, and tried to hurt her."

"I didn't know it was that serious," Dobbs said, "Look, I may have my issues with Garcia, but I would never do anything to him."

"Even if your job was in danger?" Vicki asked, deciding to take the risk.

At that moment, C.J. caught up to Angela at her room. C.J. knocked on the door and waited for her to answer. Opening the door, Angela said, "Oh, you again. Have you already found Steve?"

"No," C.J. replied, "the last time I saw Mr. Garcia was this morning, on the Lido deck."

"What can I do for you then," Angela asked, "I don't have time for a lot of questions right now. I'm very busy. If you haven't talked to him, I would appreciate it if you would leave me alone."

"What do you know about Mr. Garcia," C.J. asked casually.

"I know that he breaks his promises," Angela said angrily, "He broke his promise to negotiate our marketing co-op in good faith."

"How can you be sure of that," C.J. said, "Maybe he had an emergency and couldn't make it to the meeting."

"Well, whatever the reason," Angela scowled, "He simply didn't make it. I was counting on this deal. He's always come through before, but not this time."

"So you've worked with him on deals before," C.J. interrupted.

"Well, sure. Plenty of times," Angela replied, "But lately, I've been getting nothing but excuses."

"What would those be," C.J. asked, hoping to get more information.

"That he didn't have the funding to put into the co-op, but it was coming soon," she said, "I asked him to at least sign a contract so we could proceed with our deal, and he said he wasn't prepared to sign it yet. He's been hiding something if you ask me."

C.J. decided to reveal what she knew, "Angela...I mean Ms. Hensen...I hate to bring bad news, but it would seem Steve Garcia has disappeared from the ship. No one can find him. He's been missing since this morning. We've turned the ship upside down, but haven't been able to locate him." Ms. Hensen took a seat.

"What," she said, partially in shock, "He's missing? What's happened to him? Do you know?"

"We think he's been kidnapped," C.J. told her, "but we believe he's still on the ship. We just don't know where." C.J. sat down next to her. "Do you know anything that could help us?"

"No. My only dealings with Steve regarded the co-op agreement. I can't believe he's missing. This is terrible! If I had only known, I might not have ..."

"It's okay," C.J. said, "My friends and I are looking into this whole thing. We hope to find him soon."

Angela seemed puzzled, "What can you and your friends do?"

"I know we may seem young, but my friends and I are detectives, and we've solved many cases before. Although, nothing quite like this one." C.J. said, "Either way, we plan to get to the bottom of this. Don't worry, I'm sure we'll find him."

"Thank you for your help," Angela said as she departed. Angela didn't even look up as C.J. exited the room.

As C.J. passed by Susan's room, she noticed that the door was ajar, and she could hear Joe and Susan talking quietly together. I hope he gets more information than I did, C.J. thought, as she walked to her room.

"Susan," Joe asked, "Why do you think anyone would kidnap Steve?"

She shrugged, "I don't know. He is a wealthy and powerful man. Maybe being the CFO of an International Corporation could be part of it."

"Do you know if he has any enemies," Joe questioned.

"Steve is such a sweet man, it's hard to imagine, but I'm sure he must have some," Susan answered. "When you've climbed the ladder as high as Steve has, you're bound to have some enemies. There must be people who either want his job or don't like the fact that he is where he is. But, I'm not aware of anyone from AGM being here aside from Mr. Dobbs and Steve's boss."

Joe thought over what she had said before he asked, "What's AGM?"

"Oh. Sorry," she replied, "AGM stands for Allied Global Merchandising. It's a network of merchants from around the world."

"Well, speaking of his business, has he ever mentioned someone named Angela Hensen?"

"Yes, he's talked about her before," Susan said. "I think they were working on a Marketing Cooperative agreement. It's a deal where several companies come together, to pool their marketing moneys together, to get more visibility in a market than just one could afford."

"It sounds like you know a good deal about Steve's business with Ms. Hensen," Joe said. "Do you know anything else?"

"As I recall, Steve said he wasn't sure of the viability of Angela's company. He was willing to talk to her, but couldn't make any promises to bring her company into the co-op."

"Do you think Angela could be involved in his kidnapping," Joe questioned.

"I don't know," Susan answered inquisitively, "But, from what I understand, she really wanted this deal."

"Joe," C.J. called, "Did you get any information?"

"Susan told me a little about the business deal Steve had going with Ms. Hensen, but it's not much to go on," Joe answered. "This whole thing just doesn't add up. Have you seen Vicki lately?"

"No, she must still be talking with Mr. Dobbs," C.J. told him, "At least she's been talking with him longer than we did."

"Wait a minute," Mr. Dobbs said, "I think you're trying to accuse me of something."

"I'm sorry," Vicki replied, "I didn't mean to imply you were somehow involved. It was just a question. I'm just trying to follow up on all the leads in hopes of finding Mr. Garcia."

"I think you can leave now," Mr. Dobbs suggested. He opened the door for her and then slammed it behind her.

"What was that about," C.J. questioned, appearing from behind Vicki.

"I think I offended him when I asked if he was involved in Mr. Garcia's disappearance," Vicki replied.

"What did he say to make you ask him that question," C.J. asked.

"He didn't seem too concerned for Steve's well being," Vicki answered. "And, then he got belligerent with me the more questions I asked."

"It does seem a little weird," Joe agreed, "but it doesn't prove anything. He reacted the same way towards C.J. and me."

"Well, it doesn't matter now, does it," Vicki asked, "Mr. Dobbs just got himself put on the top of our suspect list."

Since it was turning dark outside, the three teenagers returned to their rooms and turned in, exhausted from a long day of investigating.

CHAPTER 12

It's Official!

Early the next morning, several hours before the ship set port in Halifax, Vicki and C.J. were told to report to Captain Maguire's office. "Why do you think he called us?" C.J. asked.

"I don't know," Vicki replied, "Maybe he wants to make sure we aren't getting into any trouble. Whatever it is, we're about to find out." They arrived at the Captain's office and were let in. Captain Maguire was waiting for them.

"Hello," he said, but that was the only greeting that he offered before getting straight to the point, "I wanted you to know that I'm aware of you asking a lot of questions about Mr. Garcia."

"That's correct, sir," Vicki told him.

"That is a problem," the Captain answered, pushing his chair back and standing to his feet, "I specifically instructed you kids to keep out of this. If this was a case," he leaned over towards the girls, "and it's not," rising again, "it would be a matter for our security personnel and we don't need teenagers meddling in our investigation."

"We were only trying to help," C.J. protested, "We don't see it as interfering. It is not as if we think your security is not up to the task. Steve's fiancée, Susan, asked for our help."

"I'm aware of that," Captain Maguire said, "And while I can't control what Ms. Morrow does, I can control what happens on my ship. My security will handle this."

Vicki asked, "Sir, has any of your personnel discovered anything that could lead them to the whereabouts of Mr. Garcia, if he is indeed still on this ship?"

"Not quite yet," he answered slowly, "but I know our security personnel will find him. If he's on this ship, he will be found."

"Do you have any suspects who may have kidnapped him," C.J. asked.

"We're looking into some leads," Maguire said.

"Well, sir, not only do we have several leads, we've discovered some vital information that may lead to the kidnapper."

This seemed to take the Captain by surprise. "Girls, if you know something, you should come forward with it now," the Captain said in a threatening tone.

Vicki and C.J. were not easily intimidated. C.J. spoke up, "Sir, we do have some information that might be helpful. But, we're just a little tired of being shut out of the process. If you would be willing to let us be a part of the official investigation, we would share everything we know."

"So you want some official recognition for your contribution. Is that it?" the Captain asked.

"We just want the ability to help Ms. Morrow find her fiancé without constantly being told we are meddling in adult affairs, as if we are unable to contribute," Vicki said.

"If, in fact, you have discovered some useful information, maybe we could let you be a part of our investigation," he finally admitted, "but only as long as you don't get in the way. I don't want any more reports that you are upsetting our passengers."

"Sir, before we tell you what we know, would you tell us which passenger it is that complained about us," Vicki queried.

The Captain replied, "Well, it was a Mr. Dobbs."

"I'm not surprised. He has been very hostile to our questions. We think he's been hiding something. As a matter of fact, Mr. Dobbs is our primary suspect. It turns out he and Mr. Garcia work for the same company. They were supposed to conduct a business meeting here on the ship today."

"Yeah," C.J. chimed in, "and when Vicki went to speak with him, he became quite agitated. If he cared about his boss, he should not have minded if we asked a few simple questions."

Vicki added, "Ms. Morrow told us something else as well. As it turns out, Mr. Garcia sent Susan a note before the wedding yesterday morning, telling her something was wrong, and he was concerned for her safety. It said he intended to resolve the situation, and return to explain it to her later."

"Well, ladies," the Captain stated, "That is some interesting information. But, let's not jump to any conclusions just yet. Let security look into this a little bit deeper, and we'll let you know if we find anything."

"Okay, sir," Vicki said. "Just to be clear. We now have your permission to look into Mr. Garcia's disappearance." Before the Captain could interject, she said, "... as long as we aren't bothering the other passengers." The Captain replied with a nod.

Vicki and C.J. left the office, smiling at the possibility of being involved with an official investigation, especially one outside of the little town of Sport, Maine.

"Well, that was a first," Vicki said, "It's not often that someone will admit that we have some information they can use."

C.J. nodded in agreement and then asked, "What angle should we cover next?"

"I'd like to take a look in Mr. Dobbs' room," Vicki told her, "but the problem is getting him out. He certainly won't talk to me again after what happened yesterday."

"We'll just have to wait," C.J. remarked, "I'm sure he'll leave his room eventually. We are pulling into port in a few hours. Maybe he'll go ashore. Let's go see if he's in."

As they approached Mr. Dobbs' room cautiously, they decided to see if he was home. Vicki listened at the door for a moment. "I don't hear anything. Maybe he's not here." Vicki decided to test her theory with a quiet knock.

They heard the sound of footsteps coming to answer the door and darted out of sight. Mr. Dobbs opened the door, but found no one. "That's too bad," Vicki whispered, "He's still there."

"We'll just have to try again later," C.J. replied. Vicki agreed and they went to Joe's room.

Since there seemed to be some time to kill, the group of three headed to the dance club and sat at their usual table. A waitress they had not met before came over, "Hello. Can I start you guys off with some drinks?"

"Actually," Vicki said, "We're looking for someone." She handed the waitress the photo of Steve and Susan. Have you seen him?"

"Is this Steve Garcia," the waitress asked with some surprise.

"Yes. How do you know Steve," Joe asked

The waitress responded, "He was supposed to marry my best friend Susan this morning, but it seems he stood her up at the altar."

The group looked at each other, stunned at the new information.

"I'm Natasha. I was supposed to be Susan's maid of honor. We were both pretty excited when she decided to get married onboard," Natasha informed. "At least until her fiancé disappeared."

"We've been trying to find him," Vicki said.

"So, how do you know Susan," C.J. asked.

"We used to work together at a travel agency," Natasha said, "When I got this job on the ship, we stayed in touch. Then, when she said she was getting married on a cruise ship, I couldn't believe it was the 'Crystal Palace'."

"Has Susan mentioned anything about who may have kidnapped Mr. Garcia," Vicki asked, but the waitress just shook her head.

"She doesn't want to talk about it," she said, "Now, can I get you anything? I've got to get back to work." They ordered a couple of sodas and she went to get them.

"I think we need to ask Susan some questions about her friend," Vicki said, "She's not a suspect, but we should check her out."

At that moment, the waitress returned and they quieted down. Natasha looked at them strangely for a moment and then left to take more orders.

"I guess it's time to try Mr. Dobbs' room again," Vicki said, looking at her watch. "We're going to make port in about twenty minutes. If he plans on going to Halifax, he may have already left his room. If, however, Dobbs is responsible for Steve's kidnapping, he may not leave the ship. But, I think I have an idea about how to get him out."

"How," C.J. and Joe asked together.

"I'll tell you all about it when I'm done," Vicki answered, "I'll see you guys later."

C.J. called after her, "Whatever this is, should you be doing it alone?"

Vicki replied, "Don't worry. I do my best work alone…and in secret." She slinked off.

At three o'clock the ship came to port in Halifax. Vicki had been waiting on the deck near Dobbs' corridor, to see if he went ashore. After a few minutes, she again went by his room to see if he was still occupying it. Unfortunately, he wasn't going to make it easy on her, and she had to go to plan B.

Vicki ran up several flights and made a straight line for the security office. She knocked on the door and walked in.

"I have some information for you," she told the officer behind the desk, "I have reason to believe the man in room B three-zero-three may have kidnapped Mr. Garcia, and has hidden him away somewhere on the ship. His name is Bill Dobbs." Vicki wished she had the evidence to back up her claim.

"The Captain has given me permission to investigate the disappearance, and I would like it if you could pick up Mr. Dobbs and question him concerning Mr. Garcia."

The officer sighed, "Very well. I hope he will be cooperative." He called for one of the security personnel and directed him to Mr. Dobbs' room. Vicki left and waited around the corner until the other officer returned with Mr. Dobbs.

Dobbs was acting quite irritated. "Okay, I'm going," Mr. Dobbs grunted. "What's the big idea?"

"We just want to ask you some questions," the officer replied, "It will just take a minute." Mr. Dobbs followed the officer inside while Vicki sneaked off to his room. She pulled a card out of her pocket and slipped it between the door and the jamb. After only a moment, the door opened and Vicki went inside.

She looked around the small room. A closet on one side of the room was partially opened. Lying on the bed was a briefcase. She decided to check out the closet first, but it only revealed a few items of clothing. She was unable to open the briefcase since it was securely locked.

Vicki moved to the dresser. She looked through everything, moving the contents aside as she went. She found nothing until she got to the top drawer where she found a set of keys.

She glanced at the closed briefcase on Mr. Dobbs' bed and decided to give the keys a try. After trying several keys, all of which were much too large, she found one that fit the lock perfectly. She turned it slowly until the lid popped open, revealing a bank report for the Allied Global Merchandizing Company.

Vicki picked up the report and glanced at it. Then she took another look at the briefcase, but this time at the contents underneath the report. What she found took her breath away for just a moment. Because there, covering the bottom of the case, were stacks of hundred dollar bills!

Vicki turned back to the report and glanced at the figures on the right hand column. It showed transactions to and from the corporate bank account.

According to the dates, every month on the same day, there was a large transfer of company funds to an account only identified by a number – but always the same account! The first time, ten thousand was transferred, and the next time it was twenty five thousand.

And, looking at the transaction sheet, the Assistant Financial Officer's name written on the report was William E. Dobbs. So, Vicki thought, this guy has been stealing from his own company.

Vicki noticed that pages four through seven were missing from the transaction report. She calculated in her head that the transfers still shown on the report added up to around one hundred and thirty thousand dollars. These were relatively small transfers that might have gotten lost on a report covering millions of dollars in transactions.

She was about to count the money in the case, when a sound from outside caught her attention. She quickly put the papers back inside the briefcase and the keys back in the dresser.

"Enough already," the unmistakable voice grunted, "I don't want to answer any more of your questions. Let me go." The voice down the hall belonged to Bill Dobbs!

CHAPTER 13

Halifax, Nova Scotia

Vicki was halfway to the door, when she realized that she had left the briefcase open. She ran over and slammed it shut before running out the door, locking it behind her. She willed herself to walk as she passed Mr. Dobbs in the hallway. She gave no sign of noticing or even knowing him.

Then she made her way to the dance club, where C.J. and Joe were still sitting. She sat down and caught her breath. Her friends looked at her in surprise.

"Are you okay," C.J. asked. Vicki nodded and looked up. "Where were you," C.J. continued.

"In Mr. Dobbs room," Vicki answered.

"How did you get him out," Joe asked.

"I told security that he might have some information on the case," Vicki replied, "While he was being questioned, I sneaked into his room."

"Did you find anything," C.J. cut in.

"Give me just a second," Vicki said and laughed, "Yes, I found something very helpful. I found a financial report inside his room, along with tons of cash in a brief case. There was a lot more than the ten G's we found in Steve's room."

"Are you saying what I think you are," C.J. asked. Vicki nodded.

"He's stealing money from his own company. Maybe Steve found out about it and Dobbs kidnapped him to keep it secret." Vicki looked at her friends, "Dobbs must be the man we're after."

"Did you keep any of the evidence," Joe asked.

"No," Vicki answered with some disappointment, "He returned to his room and I barely got away without being seen. Besides, you can't exactly take off with stuff like that without someone knowing that it's missing. And that could put Steve in danger."

Joe said, "It sounds like you are making some real progress. I wonder if we can take a short break and go ashore for a little while. We are supposed to be on vacation you know."

Agreeing, the group stood up and began to walk downstairs so they could get Catlin before heading to land.

"But, why would Dobbs decide to kidnap Steve on a cruise ship," Joe queried as they walked.

"I think it was just a matter of timing," Vicki said. "Someone in the company found out about the embezzlement just before their annual business meeting."

C.J. picked up the thought at that point, "Dobbs probably hoped with thousands of passengers on board, Steve would be difficult to find. And, if he could plant a fake suicide note, to throw off the ship's security team, he would be home free."

"The question is what did he do with Steve. Is he hiding him somewhere onboard," Vicki queried.

"We don't know yet," C.J. said, "But, for now, we need to tell the Captain what we've found out. The only problem is, you have this information because you broke into Mr. Dobbs' room. That might not go over well with the Captain."

"Well, if they didn't want people breaking into the staterooms, they shouldn't make it so easy," Vicki defended herself with a smooth tone in her voice, "I got in with a student I.D. card. They need better locks."

"Yeah," Joe said, "Besides, what else can we do? We are pretty sure at this point who has Garcia. We've got to do something."

"Problem is, we don't have the evidence with us," Vicki interrupted him, knocking on Catlin and Becky's door, "We can't prove anything."

Vicki was surprised to see Becky answer the door, and the rest of Vicki's family was inside.

Vicki said, "Joe, C.J., and I were headed ashore. Should we all go together?"

Vicki's dad answered, "We've just been waiting for you, Vicki."

"Yeah. As usual, the fun can't begin without Vicki," Becky added with sarcasm.

The group headed to the gangway, which was on the Plaza Deck, just above the water line.

Once off the 'Crystal Palace', the vacationers had to get used to walking on land again. Their legs had grown used to the swaying and sinking of the ship and solid ground felt almost foreign.

The minute the group stepped off, they knew that the brochure hadn't been lying. The scenery in Halifax was as breathtaking as it had said, with the ocean lapping against the shoreline.

Various shops lined the edge of the wharf, completing the boardwalk area. Vicki could see crowds of people milling about here and there, entering clubs and cafes, with music floating through the air from a nearby park.

"Look at all the cute little shops," Catlin exclaimed, "Anyone want to go look around with me?" Becky readily volunteered and the girls set off, after making sure that their cell phones were on at the insistence of Vicki's parents, and being reminded that the ship would leave again in three hours.

Vicki, C.J. and Joe opted to check out the waterfront and then the downtown area.

"Make sure to at least attend one educational attraction," Vicki's father told them, "This town is chock full of them and I think you'll find some of the history to be engaging."

The three strolled along the waterfront, occasionally pausing at small shops along the way.

About a half-mile down the waterfront, the teens caught sight of the local museum and decided to go inside. It would serve as both an educational venture and shade from the hot and humid sun.

As they walked around, only one exhibit caught all of their eyes.

"I didn't know that Halifax had anything to do with the Titanic," Vicki commented as she studied the exhibit sign.

"Yes, you did," C.J. told her, "We studied it in our history class sophomore year. Or don't you remember Mr. Feldenhoffer's lecture?"

"Oh yeah," Vicki exclaimed, "I just didn't put two and two together." She was remembering the interesting lecture their history teacher presented on the Titanic.

He had the students arrive at class in period costume clothing from the early 1900s. Then he went through the event, engaging the teenagers in the real life tragedy. Weeks before, he made them write numerous journal entries as a make-believe passenger on the ship, up to the horrifying moment when the Titanic began to sink. On that fateful class day, they had shared their pretend entries with the rest of the students.

"It says here that Halifax sent out three of their own ships to recover the bodies," C.J. remarked, reading from a pamphlet she had picked up outside the exhibit, "There are three cemeteries in this area for the one hundred and fifty unclaimed victims."

"Three," Vicki couldn't keep the disturbing images out of her head. "And that was just for one ship?" She looked over at C.J.

C.J. immediately understood what was going through Vicki's mind, and her eyes met Vicki's determinedly. "There won't be another victim to add to the list. We will find Mr. Garcia."

One of the most significant artifacts on display was an original deck chair. It appeared to be in pristine condition. Sitting by itself, it was a reminder of the fifteen hundred people who lost their lives.

The one piece, though, that really drove home the event was the log from the communications officer on the Titanic. He recorded each wireless message, beginning with the initial strike against the iceberg. It recorded every detail leading to the eventual sinking of the "unsinkable" ship. It was a chilling first hand account that affected all who read it.

The teenagers finished going through the exhibit before moving back outside. Heading downtown, they observed the bustle of the city before deciding what to do next. Joe finally pointed out a café down the street and suggested they stop for an early dinner. The girls quickly agreed with his idea.

Ordering three deli sandwiches and sodas, the teenagers sat down at a booth and began to eat. It wasn't long however, before Vicki turned to look as the main entrance swung open, and in walked Bill Dobbs.

"What's he doing here?" Vicki asked.

C.J. and Joe watched as the man ordered at the front counter.

"I think it's pretty clear what he's doing here, Vicki," Joe replied, "He's human too." Though the statement was made to be funny, Vicki barely even acknowledged it, probably due to the fact that being in the same location with the man in question seemed a bit too coincidental.

"Looks like you didn't have to lure him out after all," C.J. whispered, "We could have just waited for him to leave."

"I didn't think he would," Vicki defended herself, "As far as I was concerned at the time, it was my only shot to get him out. But maybe he discovered we went ashore, and thought it was safe to venture out."

"Or maybe he's here for other reasons," Joe stated.

"You think he's been following us," C.J. asked, though she looked uncertain about the question, "It seems too obvious if he is."

"I wouldn't doubt it," Vicki said, "There are several cafes on this street and he chooses to eat at this one, where we just happen to be."

"He sure is ordering a lot for one person," C.J. commented, as the woman working the front counter was still figuring out his total.

C.J. thought for a moment, glancing at Mr. Dobbs from the corner of her eye. She finally returned her attention to Vicki and Joe, but when she spoke, it was in a whisper.

"I know what we need to do," C.J. stated, and her two friends crowded closer, "We need to check anyplace Dobbs could be hiding Mr. Garcia on the ship. Empty staterooms, storage holds, lifeboats, anyplace where there aren't people."

"That sounds like a good idea," Vicki agreed, "Let's tell the Captain what we know and see if he will spare some security men to help us search the ship and get us into some of the off-limits areas." She turned to Joe, "We'll need you and Catlin to help out."

"No problem," Joe said and smiled, "I'll get Catlin and meet you at Captain Maguire's office." He left, and found Catlin browsing with Becky in the deluge of shops. He quickly explained the situation and Catlin turned to leave, shifting her bag of souvenirs to her other hand.

"Wait a minute," Becky stopped the two in their tracks, "You can't just leave me by myself." She looked at Catlin with a mix of disappointment and anger.

Catlin glanced over at Joe, "I guess she could…" She shifted her gaze to Becky again, "Look, I'll clue you in to what's happening if you won't cause any trouble."

Becky sighed but agreed, then used her cell phone to call her parents and went to meet them at the waterfront.

Joe and Catlin met with Vicki and C.J. back onboard, and then proceeded to the

Captain's office a few minutes later. They were there half an hour before the departure time.

Vicki knocked before walking inside the room. "Enter," came the stern voice of the Captain. Upon seeing the faces of the four teens, the Captain shook his head and said, "Ms. Silver. What can I do for you now?"

"Sir, we've recently come across some startling new evidence. I can't tell you how I know this," Vicki started cautiously, "but Mr. Dobbs is the one who has been embezzling money from his company, possibly up to one hundred and thirty thousand dollars worth."

The Captain replied, "That's very interesting. I will need to see some evidence before we can arrest him, though."

"Sir, I understand that," Vicki stated. "But right now my biggest concern is finding Mr. Garcia. It's obvious he isn't in any of the occupied rooms. We need access to every part of the ship, even the unoccupied sections. Could you spare a few security personnel to escort us around?"

"All of our security personnel are on shore duty. They are busy checking everyone as they re-enter the ship," the Captain said.

"In that case, would it be possible for us to borrow some uniforms," C.J. asked the Captain.

"With uniforms, passengers wouldn't think twice if they saw us looking around different parts of the ship," Vicki explained.

"Okay," Captain Maguire consented, "But remember to tell security if you find anything suspicious. You can only borrow them for the day. Bring them back as soon as you can. There's a few back here, let me get them for you."

Captain Maguire went into another room and returned shortly with four worker's uniforms. They were white outfits with gold buttons on the front. He handed one to each of them, "Let me know if you find anything."

The four teenagers took turns in the only restroom near the bridge, and changed into the uniforms. The girls were not happy with the fit, but knew there was little they could do about it. Catlin cinched her uniform with a gold cord around the waistline. She was determined to be the most stylish ship's worker in uniform.

The group immediately began searching rooms. They each took a section of the ship. Catlin got the Baja Deck where Mr. Dobbs was staying. He didn't know who she was and shouldn't think anything of her sudden appearance.

They all set out to work, not knowing if they would find anything of importance in any of the rooms they searched. C.J. took the Caribe Deck. Joe took the Emerald deck and Vicki took the Dolphin deck.

Vicki knocked on the door of one of the larger staterooms and waited until a woman who looked to be around fifty opened the door.

"Hello," the lady said, surprised to find a teenager outside her door, "What can I do for you?"

"Hello, ma'am," Vicki said as she peered past the woman to visually examine her room, "I am with the ship's staff. I was wondering how you are enjoying the cruise?"

"It's wonderful," the lady gushed, "I have never been on a cruise like this before. There's everything here. There's restaurants and spas and..."

Vicki interrupted, "Ma'am, have you seen or heard anything out of the ordinary since the beginning of the trip? Anything that might have concerned you... especially on the first day?"

"No, nothing that I can recall," the lady answered with a puzzled frown.

"Well, thanks for your help," Vicki said and waited while the woman closed the door. Moving to the next door, Vicki knocked again.

C.J. moved down the row of doors before her. "Hello," she called and knocked on the next door. A teenage boy answered.

"What," he asked, "Do you want something?" He looked down at her.

"Hi, I'm with the crew. We are searching for a missing passenger. Have you heard or seen anything strange since the trip started?" she looked up at him. He seemed to think for a minute before answering.

"Nope. I haven't seen anything out of the ordinary," he said. "It's pretty quiet down here, you know?"

"Well, thank you," C.J. replied and he closed the door behind her. Well, he was no help, she thought to herself. I wish there was one clue that we could find.

Joe walked to the next door and knocked. A teenage girl opened the door. When she saw Joe standing there, she quickly started to close it. He stopped her hastily, but restrained himself from actually putting out his hand to stop the closing door, as to keep from startling her further, "Wait," he said, "I just want to ask you a question. It won't take long."

"Well," the girl said, looking around, though she finished putting the chain in place, "I guess it'll be okay. What do you want to know?"

"Have you heard or seen anything strange since you came on board," he asked. The girl took a step back.

"Why do you want to know that for," she asked, looking at Joe curiously.

Joe replied, "The Captain wants to make sure all of our guests are enjoying their trip."

"Well, now that I think about it," the girl said, "I did hear some strange sounds when I first came on board yesterday morning."

"Where were they coming from," Joe asked, taking interest.

"Down the hallway somewhere," she answered while gesturing towards the aft end of the corridor, "They were very strange. They sounded like something heavy being dragged across the floor. Then I heard some loud thumping noises. I didn't know what they were and I didn't dare look to find out."

"Thank you. You were a lot of help," Joe said to the girl.

"No problem," the girl called as she closed the door.

Catlin knocked on Mr. Dobbs' door. She heard a sound inside and took a quick step back. Mr. Dobbs opened the door and looked at the teenager in front of him.

"What do you want," he asked, obviously not wanting to talk.

Catlin tried to smile, "We were wondering how you were enjoying your trip, sir," she said, hoping to sound convincing.

"It could be better," he answered, "Tell your boss that I want those kids to stop bothering me." He started to close the door, when Catlin interrupted him.

"I am so sorry about that," Catlin said, "I will be sure to tell him. But, is everything else okay, sir?"

He sighed and looked down at her, "Yes, everything is fine. I'm just tired of all those kids asking questions. Now, will you please leave?"

"Wait a minute," she continued, "Is there anything that I can do to make your trip more enjoyable?"

"Yes, there is something you can do," he said, "You can leave me alone. Why are you asking me all these questions?" He eyed her suspiciously and she took a quick step back. "I have never seen you with the crew here before. Are you new?"

Catlin didn't answer and he glared at her, "I'm beginning to wonder about you," he said, "I don't think you really work here."

She still didn't answer and he stepped forward, raising his voice, "Wait a minute. Are you with those kids who were here earlier? You're with them, aren't you? You're spying on me! That's why you're here, isn't it? Are you with the crew or not?"

CHAPTER 14

Attempted Escape

Time passed by slowly in the silence. To Steve, the hours dragged by and he had no way of knowing how much time had passed. The man responsible for his kidnapping came by every few hours, with some food and occasionally water to drink. Otherwise, the man showed no regard for Steve's well being.

There were intervals when Steve slept, as a person could only stay awake so long with their own thoughts. As was to be expected, though, Steve never woke feeling refreshed, but rather grew more groggy and sore, due to the hard floor and the inability to move freely.

When he was awake, though, Steve's thoughts were of Susan and how she must be coping. Other than that, his time was spent trying to piece together whose voice it was that he heard every day.

Once, Steve thought he heard footsteps outside the door, so he attempted to call out through the tape over his mouth. However, it had turned out to be his captor. So, now Steve had a gag in his mouth under the tape, to muffle his voice even more. And, whenever he was alone, his hands were bound behind his back, which made any attempt to escape almost impossible.

CHAPTER 15

Quarantine

"Yes," Catlin finally answered, daring herself to look up at Mr. Dobbs, as if direct eye contact would convince him of her innocence, "I'm here under the direction of the Captain, to ask all the passengers on this deck, if they need anything to make their stay onboard more enjoyable." She nearly ran out of breath before finishing. She could see that Mr. Dobbs was still having a hard time believing her.

"Is that so," he asked. He calmed down and looked at her silently.

"Yes, sir," Catlin said, nodding. Catlin motioned towards the desk in Mr. Dobbs room, and said, "I'll ring the bridge on your phone if you like, and you can ask the Captain yourself."

"That won't be necessary. I'm sorry to have sounded suspicious," Mr. Dobbs said, stepping back and allowing the door to open wide, showing that he was no threat, "I thought you were one of those nosy kids who keeps coming over here. I just assumed. You do look around their age."

"That's okay, sir," Catlin said, "I'll tell my boss to ask them not to bug you anymore. Have a good day." She turned around and walked away. She could hear the sound of the door closing behind her.

It's a good thing he doesn't know the truth, she thought; her heart was racing with alarm. He wouldn't be happy to know that I really am one of those kids. She forced herself to walk slowly, in case Mr. Dobbs happened to be observing her actions through the door viewer.

Catlin walked down the corridor, and took the elevator to the Emerald Deck, where they had agreed to meet.

"So, Catlin. How is Mr. Dobbs these days," Vicki asked.

"He started yelling at me," Catlin said, laughing nervously, "He thought that I was with that group of kids that was spying on him."

"Good thing you weren't," C.J. said with a smile. "At least you kept your cover. We can't go anywhere near his room, after what Vicki did."

"Okay," Vicki said, "So what did you guys find out?"

"Nothing," C.J. replied. They all turned to Joe.

"When I was down on the Emerald Deck, someone said they heard strange sounds shortly after arriving yesterday morning," he said, "which seems to coincide with the time that Mr. Garcia went missing. All she said was that it was coming from down the corridor where several of the unoccupied areas are. I think they are mechanical rooms. It's not much to go on. How about you, C.J.?"

"I didn't find out anything new," C.J. admitted, "Nobody on the Caribe Deck mentioned anything out of the ordinary. It sounds like you got the most interesting lead of the bunch."

"It might not mean anything, though," Joe said.

Vicki offered, "We could check with Captain Maguire, and see which rooms on the Emerald deck are empty. That might get us closer to finding out where the sounds came from."

The group of teenagers went to Captain Maguire's office and found Jonathan Burns, the steward, manning the desk.

"Hey, Jonathan," Vicki called out. "Did the Captain mention to you that he is letting us investigate Mr. Garcia's disappearance?"

"Actually, he did mention that," Jonathan said. "I was surprised, to say the least."

"Listen, we received a report of some strange sounds on the Emerald Deck yesterday morning. Do you know which rooms on that deck are empty? We would like to check them out."

Jonathan replied, "Actually, that deck only has one room that isn't occupied; room E three-twenty-seven. And it's only vacant because we had to move someone out after a complaint."

"What do you mean," Vicki asked.

"Well, don't let this get around, but we had to quarantine the room. A passenger reported it was making him sick. We get reports like that sometimes, ever since the Norovirus scare on cruise ships a few years back."

"Why wasn't the room marked, quarantined," Vicki asked. "It might have been a lead."

"That's not the sort of thing you want to get around on a cruise ship," Jonathan replied. "Some passengers can be easily influenced by suggestion. It's best to keep those things quiet. We only closed off the room as a precaution. There is probably nothing wrong with it."

"Then you won't mind if we check it out," Vicki said.

"I guess it would be okay, seeing as how the Captain has cleared you guys to investigate Mr. Garcia's disappearance," Jonathan said reluctantly.

He hit a few keys on his computer keyboard, and then fed a key card through a slot. Handing it to Vicki, Jonathan said, "Here you go. This will get you into the room."

"Thanks, that will be a big help," Vicki said. "And, thanks for the information."

Vicki added, "Hey, we are all going to lunch at the dance club. Would you care to join us?"

"I guess that would be okay. I'm due for my lunch break," Jonathan said. The group cleared the office, and he locked the door behind.

The gang found their table, and each ordered something to drink.

Vicki didn't waste any time asking Jonathan more questions. "So, Jonathan, what else do you know about Mr. Garcia?"

"I don't know much about Steve. He usually stayed in his room. You see, he's been on more than one cruise with us."

"Really," Vicki asked, "So, he almost never left his room at all? Why do you think that is?"

"I don't know," Jonathan answered, "I guess he only really came for business trips now and then. It was a way for him to relax. I just assumed that he liked being alone."

"Didn't you find that a little strange," C.J. cut in, "Don't most people come on cruises to have fun?"

"Usually they do," he replied, "For some people, it's just a reason to get away from the office for a while." He shrugged, "Some people are just like that."

"But, didn't he ever bring his fiancée before," asked Catlin.

"No, he always came alone. I guess it was before he met Ms. Morrow."

"That might be it," Vicki said, sounding only half convinced.

"Guys," Vicki said, "after we eat. Let's talk to Susan again, and see if she knows about Steve's previous trips onboard.

The group ordered their food, and chatted while they waited. It wasn't long before their order arrived.

After just a few bites, Vicki asked Jonathan another question, "I can't believe I didn't ask this before, but do you happen to remember who the passenger was that said room E three-twenty-seven made them sick?"

"Actually, I do remember. Oddly enough, it was Bill Dobbs."

CHAPTER 16

Intruder

Everyone stopped mid bite, stood up, and in unison headed for the door. That is, everyone except for Catlin. She was so distracted with Jonathan, she didn't realize the implication of what he had said.

"You know, I haven't seen the whole ship yet," Catlin told him, "Would you mind showing me around a bit? I would like to know more about it."

"Sure," Jonathan said, sounding a little nervous, "What would you like to see first? We have all sorts of activities."

"I don't care," Catlin replied, "I just want to see everything."

Vicki, Joe, and C.J. left the club. They headed towards the Emerald Deck. After a short elevator ride, the group quickly found room E three-twenty-seven.

Vicki pulled the keycard from her pocket, and swiped it in the reader. It did not respond. She tried it again, several times.

"Guys," Vicki said, "Either Jonathan gave us the wrong card, or this reader is broken."

Joe said, "Either way, we need in that room."

Vicki tried several things to get through the lock, but to no avail. Finally the girls looked at Joe, and motioned towards the door.

C.J. said, "Okay, Joe. Now it's your turn."

Vicki added, "I'd do it, but I wouldn't want to show you up."

Joe smiled, and made an attempt to kick in the door. It held firm.

Joe smiled again, this time a bit strained. Again he kicked the door, and again. Each time putting more force behind it. Finally the doorjamb split at the lock, and the three were able to push it open.

Vicki chided, "Maybe next time, I'll do it myself." Joe gave her a smirk, but didn't argue since he was just a little out of breath.

Vicki noticed, not only did the doorframe splinter at the lock, but shards of the door were still stuck to the frame.

"It looks like someone glued the door shut. They really didn't want anyone to get in here," Vicki said. "No wonder it was so hard to break down."

Joe felt vindicated, but was busy searching the room for any clues.

C.J. asked, "Do you think someone on the ship's crew glued the door shut, because of the threat of quarantine?"

Vicki said, "There's no way. You heard Jonathan. They thought it was a false alarm. Dobbs must have returned to this room, and done it himself. He probably still had the keycard."

"Well, it looks like this is what he was hiding," Joe said.

The girls turned their attention to where Joe was standing.

Joe had pulled back the covers to the bed, and on the pillow was a small bloodstain.

"That could be from a head wound," Vicki said. "In a way, that's good. There isn't a lot of blood, and it it belongs to Steve, at least he was still onboard and alive."

C.J. added, "It looks pretty old. Whoever it was has probably not been in this room for at least twenty-four hours. And, he probably changed clothes while he was here, too."

Vicki looked at her friend strangely, "C.J., how did you surmise that?"

C.J. looked in the direction of the closet, "Because there's a black tuxedo in the closet."

Vicki walked to the closet to get a closer look. "That's the one. I recognize the boutonniere on the lapel. It's for sure then, Steve was in this room."

Vicki continued, "Dobbs must have held Steve here for a short while, and then moved him somewhere else."

"Joe," Vicki said, "Would you mind getting this information to the Captain? They need to arrest Dobbs immediately. C.J. and I will speak to Susan." Joe agreed, and the group split up.

The girls went back up to the Aloha Deck, and straight for Susan's room. They heard music inside as they knocked. "I'm coming," Susan's voice called and the music shut off. She looked surprised to see her new friends. "Hello..."

"Susan," Vicki began, "We have some news. If what we found means what we think it does, Steve is onboard and still alive."

"That's great," Susan said excited. "What did you find?" she asked.

"We were just in a vacant room that had some evidence that Steve may have been held there for a short time. We don't know where he is right at this moment, but we are getting closer." This information seemed to be more concerning to Susan than comforting.

"Don't worry," C.J. said, "We hope to find him soon. I'm sure Steve is okay."

"You don't know that," Susan said shakily, "What could they have done with him? There's no sign that they are going to let him go. I thought they would have sent a ransom note by now. He does have a lot of money."

"We don't think that are holding him for ransom," Vicki said, "We don't have the evidence to show you just yet, but I think we know why he was kidnapped. We believe one of his business partners is trying to cover his tracks long enough to get off the ship. I don't think he intends to harm Steve."

"I hope that's the case," Susan said, trying to sound cheerful about the news, "Let's just hope it all turns out okay."

Vicki and C.J. left quietly and walked down the hallway to their rooms.

"We need to change out of these uniforms. If we hang around in these things too much longer, the other passengers will get suspicious."

"We do look kind of strange standing out here in these," C.J. said, looking at herself, "We've been so busy, I forgot about them."

"C.J.," Vicki asked as they entered their cabin.

"What," her friend questioned, sitting on her bed.

"I've been wondering. Why would Mr. Dobbs steal from his own company?"

"Right," C.J. answered, "I have been wondering the same thing. He's probably making enough money as the assistant CFO at AGM. There's no reason for him to steal."

"Maybe he's one of those people that can't get enough," Vicki suggested, "He wants everything and is never satisfied."

"That might be it," C.J. agreed, "But wouldn't the head of the company notice that their money was being siphoned off?" Vicki shrugged.

Vicki and C.J. changed into some jeans and t-shirts before leaving to find Joe.

Joe made it to the Captain's Office and found Jonathan. "Jonathan," Joe said, "We went to room E three-twenty-seven and found evidence that someone was being held in that room. We believe Mr. Dobbs was holding Steve Garcia in there, but now he has moved him."

Jonathan asked, "What did you find?"

"We found what we believe to be Steve's tuxedo. Vicki recognized it from the time she saw him on the Lido Deck. And, there was some blood on the pillow," Joe answered.

Jonathan thought a moment, and said, "The only people that should have had access to that room was security and myself. Although, Mr. Dobbs may have kept his keycard."

Joe continued, "What's more, is that the door had been glued shut...um...you'll have to forgive me, but we had to break the door down to see if Steve was in there."

Jonathan said, "I understand. I'll inform the Captain what you've discovered. He will have to authorize us to arrest Mr. Dobbs."

After a few moments in the Captain's office, Jonathan returned with a ship's warrant for Mr. Dobbs.

Jonathan, Joe, and two security officers headed for the Baja deck to capture Mr. Dobbs.

When they arrived at his room, Jonathan knocked. "Mr. Dobbs, it's security. We have a warrant for your arrest. Please open up."

There was no answer.

Jonathan pulled out a master keycard from his pocket, and swiped it in the reader. The door unlocked and swung open. Joe stepped in but found no one home. He noticed that everything had been removed from the room.

The infamous briefcase was gone, as well as all of Dobbs' clothing. Dobbs was gone.

Vicki was just slipping her arms into her jacket, when a peculiar sound reached her ears. A thin card slipped between the door and the lock. The cabin door softly creaked open behind the girls. A hand reached inside and suddenly the lights in the room were switched off. Vicki and C.J. turned around quickly to see the shadow of a man standing in the doorway.

The darkness concealed his features, making it impossible to identify him. But, there was just enough light silhouetting the intruder to clearly see the shape of a gun ... and then he pointed it in their direction!

CHAPTER 17

Kidnapped

Vicki and C.J. decided to take action while the lights were out. The intruder probably didn't know it, but sometimes darkness gives the advantage to those being attacked. They each took a side and prepared to jump him. Before they could though, the person spoke up, "Don't try anything," he said, "I will use this." He moved the gun in emphasis.

"What are you doing," Vicki asked him from a corner of the room. Without him knowing, she removed an object from around her neck and dropped it on the ground.

In the next second, her hand closed around the blue velvet ring box on her dresser. She quickly slipped it into one of her inside jacket pockets.

"I know what you've discovered," he said, "And, I can't let you tell the authorities." Vicki looked over at C.J., hoping that she had a way to stall for time.

"How did you know it was us," C.J. asked.

"Who else on this ship has been snooping around, and putting their noses where they don't belong," he replied. "That's your answer."

"What are you planning to do with us," Vicki asked, "You can't do anything without someone getting suspicious. There's already been one disappearance. Two more will just assure them that something's going on."

"Let them think what they want," the man said, "As long as I can get off this ship before you are discovered, who cares?"

"We aren't the only people who know about this." C.J. told him, "My friend has gone to report this to security and you'll get caught."

"I'm not worried about security. They think this whole thing is a wild goose chase. They've been humoring you. You're just kids," the man replied, "Right now, I'm worried about you two girls saying something to the cops on the mainland. Now, move! And stop talking!"

Reluctantly, the girls were forced to walk ahead of him. He motioned for them to enter the elevator, and then he pushed the button for the Emerald Deck. The girls wondered if he intended to take them to room E three-twenty-seven.

Once they exited the elevator, he said "Turn here." They traveled down the corridor, past room E three-twenty-seven, and then proceeded to an unoccupied portion of the ship used for mechanical equipment and storage.

He led them to a small, cramped room, and forced them inside. He pulled a pile of rope from the corner and tossed it to Vicki, "Tie up your friend here." Vicki looked at C.J. hesitantly. "Do it," he repeated.

Vicki dropped down and whispered, "Sorry about this C.J." She loosely wrapped it around her friend's hands.

"Do it tight," the man ordered, "I don't want any slack in those ropes. Vicki sighed and tightly wound the rope around C.J.'s hands.

"It's okay," C.J. whispered back, "We don't really have a choice here." Vicki finished and the man inspected it closely.

"Good job," he said to Vicki and pulled another coil out, "Sit down," he ordered her. She didn't move. He sighed and started towards her. She used the time to think of a plan. Vicki spun around quickly with a high kick.

He was a step ahead of her. He seemed to think that was exactly what she had planned and grabbed hold of her ankle. Then he pushed her back. "Sit." He tightly wound the rope around her wrists. The whole time, Vicki glared at him, "We don't have any hard feelings now, do we?" He laughed.

"Hey buddy," he said, motioning to a figure in one corner of the room, "You have some company." The two girls heard muffled sounds from the figure. Then their captor tied their feet together. Then he tied cloths over their mouths, so they couldn't yell out. He quickly went to the door and shut it, leaving them in the dark.

"One more thing," he said, sticking his head in, "Even if you manage to get free, which I doubt you will. This door is a security door. You won't be able to pick it." He shut it again.

Vicki and C.J. sat quietly in the lightless room for a moment, before getting adjusted to the darkness.

What are we going to do now, Vicki thought. Vicki tried several things to loosen the ropes around her wrists, but only accomplished to bruise them. C.J. wasn't able to do any better. The kidnapper had made sure their ropes wouldn't budge. She tried hurriedly to think of a plan. She knew that C.J. was trying to think of one, too.

CHAPTER 18

Missing in Action

Joe, Jonathan, and the security detail walked down to Vicki and C.J.'s room and knocked. The door instantly opened, revealing an empty room. "Hello," Joe called, "Is anyone here?" But there was no answer.

Next Joe woke Catlin and walked over to Susan's room.

Joe asked, "Susan, have you seen Vicki or C.J.?"

Susan replied, "Yes, they were here just a little while ago. They said something about finding evidence about Steve. I think they went back to their room. Is something wrong," Susan asked.

"I don't know yet," Joe answered, "They weren't in their room just now, and we can't find our suspect."

Susan said, "I hope the girls are okay. Let me know when you find them, okay." Joe acknowledged and the group left.

"Jonathan," Joe said. "Thanks for your help. If you don't mind, I'm going to look around and see if I can find Vicki and C.J."

Jonathan replied, "We'll look around as well. If we find Dobbs, or the girls, we'll let you know."

Catlin glanced at Joe sympathetically before turning and walking down the hallway with Jonathan. Joe decided to search the girls' room for clues.

He reached their room and pushed the door open again. Joe looked around and spotted something on the floor.

He recognized it instantly. It was the golden cross necklace he had given to Vicki. He knew she almost never took it off.

He wondered if it meant anything, or if it just fell off the night table by accident. Other than that, the room was empty. He stepped outside and back towards his room.

"Ready for the rest of the tour," Jonathan asked Catlin.

"Not exactly the kind of tour I was expecting," Catlin said.

"Maybe later I can show you some more restaurants and even the game rooms," he replied. "Besides the dance club, I've heard that is the best place to hang out."

"Sounds good," Catlin answered and followed him down one level of stairs, "Do you hang out there often?"

"Not often. Only on my breaks," he answered. "Which happens to be three times a day," he chuckled.

Catlin responded, "I've never really been into games very much. But, I'm willing to learn."

"Hey Jonathan," she asked. When he turned to her, she continued, "This is a large ship and I was just wondering, are there any kind of secret passages or empty storage holds onboard?"

"Secret passages," Jonathan laughed, "I don't think there's anything like that here. Why do you ask?"

"I just wonder, if Mr. Dobbs did kidnap Steve Garcia, maybe he could be holding him in an unoccupied area of the ship?"

"There are plenty of those," he replied, "Like all ships, there are storage areas, mechanical rooms, and engine rooms. That sort of thing. But I don't really venture into those areas very much. They tend to be noisy, and are kept out of sight and sound of the passengers."

"So," Catlin said, "That might be a good place to hide someone?"

Jonathan just raised his eyebrow at her, "But, if I don't know those areas very well, how would a kidnapper know where they are?"

"Good point," Catlin agreed.

Joe turned back down the hallway. He stopped as he saw a figure enter his room. He decided to stay calm and wait for whomever it was to leave. The figure might leave a clue as to where his friends were.

He ducked into an alcove and watched from a distance.

Joe heard the sound of footsteps fading away and cautiously stepped back out into the hall. The figure was gone, so he felt that it was safe to enter his room.

The place was a mess. Not that it mattered, Joe wasn't the cleanest person, but he could tell some of his stuff had been moved. It appeared the intruder didn't leave any clues, so he decided this was as good a time as any to go and talk to Vicki's parents.

CHAPTER 19

Moments from Freedom

C.J. was trying to think of something they could do, besides just sitting there frustrated from being held against their will. She knew that Vicki had a pocketknife in her back pocket, but her friend wouldn't be able reach it. The kidnapper had bound Vicki's hands too tightly.

Vicki leaned back against the wall and worked on calming down. She guessed that the other figure in the room was Steve Garcia, but none of the captives could speak to each other. She had to find a way to escape.

C.J. looked over at Vicki, who appeared to be thinking as well. Vicki looked back at her with the same blank expression. They had been there all night, trying anything possible to loosen the ropes, but nothing worked.

C.J. looked around the room. It was small and crammed full of broken items. Nothing would be of help to them.

The first thing she had to do was uncover her mouth. Maybe she could explain some things to Vicki that way. She slowly brought her knees up and brushed off the gag she was wearing.

"Vicki," she whispered. Vicki looked up. Soon enough, Vicki had hers off, too. "What should we do?"

"Well, I'm sure yelling for help would be useless," Vicki whispered back, "No one could hear us down here."

"Do you think you can reach your pocketknife," C.J. asked in an undertone.

"I don't think so," Vicki answered, "I can't move my hands down far enough to get into my pocket."

"There must be something we can do," C.J. said, "Can you at least try one more time?"

"Okay," Vicki said, "I'll try again."

C.J. watched as her friend slowly reached for her back pocket. Vicki knew she shouldn't be carrying a pocketknife, but it sometimes came in handy. Vicki was about an inch away from reaching her pocket when she stopped.

"I can't get it, C.J.," Vicki said, "I wish that I had left more clues for Joe to find us with."

"What are you talking about," C.J. asked.

"Before we were kidnapped, I managed to get my necklace off and leave it on the floor. He didn't notice because it was so dark. Before I could do anything else, he ordered us out."

"Do you see anything of use in here," C.J. asked. Vicki shook her head and C.J. sighed. "Great, so we're basically stuck here."

She heard Vicki shifting around and then a muffled cry, "What's wrong," C.J. immediately asked.

"There's a nail or something sticking out of the wall," Vicki replied, "When I shifted around, I hit it."

"Vicki," C.J. exclaimed, not even bothering to keep her voice down, "That's it. Can you get your hands to the nail? You can cut yourself free."

"I'll try," Vicki said and maneuvered her hands up. Vicki moved her hands around until she felt the nail behind her. "I think I found it."

"All right," C.J. said, trying not to yell a second time, "How long do you think it'll take you?"

"I don't know," Vicki replied, "It's pretty sturdy, but these ropes are thick. It will take me some time."

Vicki could tell that the rope was fraying and worked harder. Little by little it came undone, but it was exhausting work.

"Are you done yet," C.J. asked some ten minutes later.

"Hold on," Vicki said, "I've almost got it undone. Just a few more times and I should be free." Seconds later, C.J. heard the rope break.

"Yes," C.J. said with a sigh. She watched impatiently as Vicki untied her feet and moved toward her. Vicki pulled out her pocketknife and set to work.

A while later, C.J. was free also. "Go help the other guy," C.J. told her.

Vicki moved over to untie the other figure. She immediately removed the blind-fold and recognized him as Steve Garcia. His eyes were wide open, and almost frantic. Although the girls had been searching for him for days, he had no recollection of the two girls he passed by on the Lido deck on the first day of the cruise.

After a moment of Vicki working on the ropes around Steve's hands, they were freed and he reached for the tape on his mouth. In an exhausted voice he said, "Thanks. I didn't think I was ever going to be free again."

"You're Steve Garcia, right," Vicki asked, and he looked at her, startled.

"How do you know my name?"

"We met your fiancée, Susan. When we heard about your disappearance, we offered to help find you," Vicki answered him, sawing through the final bit of rope surrounding his ankles, "We're amateur detectives that just happened to be on a cruise."

C.J. made her way over and sat beside them, "Susan is very worried about you, you know?"

"I knew she would be having a hard time with my disappearance," Steve said, "How is she taking it?"

"As well as can be expected," Vicki replied, "She's extremely worried about you."

Vicki then pulled the ring box out of her pocket, "I've been waiting a long time to give this back to you. I think this is yours."

Steve took it from her hand in amazement, "Where did you get this?" He closed his eyes, and clinched it to his chest. "Thank you."

"You dropped it on the Lido Deck," Vicki answered, "We kind of ran across each other's paths. I tried to give it back earlier, but you seemed a little preoccupied. After that, I kind of followed you around, trying to find out what was going on."

"You followed me," Steve asked.

"It's an occupational hazard, being detectives and all," Vicki told him, then smiled shyly, "though we weren't officially investigating at the time."

"Then why," Steve asked.

"Curiosity, I guess," Vicki answered with a shrug.

"So, you and Susan were supposed to get married, right," C.J. interrupted, more of a statement than a comment.

"Yes, we were," he agreed, "She must have explained that to you."

"Yeah, she also told us that her father doesn't like you very much," Vicki told him.

"That's a nice way to put it," Steve answered, "That man hates me. He had to know exactly where we were going when we went on dates, which is reasonable. But she was nearly thirty. Not exactly a child anymore," he paused for a moment, "Hey, what are your names?"

"I'm Vicki Silver and this is C.J. Summers," Vicki told him.

"Hey, I think I've heard of you girls," Steve replied after a second, "Aren't you the girls that solved that diamond case in Sport, Maine? I must say that I'm impressed."

C.J. said in an excited tone, "Hey, Vicki. He's heard of us. We're famous."

"Now's not the time for that," Vicki said, "We need to get out of here. Our friends will be worried. Joe's probably out looking for us by now."

C.J. stated, turning to Vicki, "That door might as well be steel."

"We have escaped from rooms with steel doors before," Vicki pointed out.

"Yeah, but then we had lock pick kits," C.J. replied, "I didn't exactly have time to grab mine before we were forced out of the room."

"Let's try the door anyway," Vicki said. Standing up and walking over to the door, she said, "Is there anything in this room that we can wedge in-between this space?"

"I don't know," C.J. answered.

"Just see if you can find something to put in here," Vicki said with exasperation. C.J. returned a few minutes later with a metal bar in her hand.

"I pulled it out from under a bed," C.J. told her.

"This will work great," Vicki said and pushed it into the space. "This should at least give us some tension."

"Maybe just enough so you can get the door open," C.J. agreed, "Let's just hope that man doesn't come back while we're doing this."

"Don't even say that," Vicki said.

"If you can push on the bar," C.J. suggested, "Maybe I can use your pocketknife to push the locking mechanism back."

Steve offered to help, but the girls could tell he was too exhausted from his ordeal to be much assistance.

Vicki stepped over to the other side and pushed as hard as she could on the bar as her friend worked on the lock. Finally, after what seemed like fifteen minutes, the two girls heard a click, meaning that the door was unlocked.

The two friends gave each other silent high-fives and started to open the door when footsteps sounded outside. They left the door in its closed position, being careful not to lock it. The footsteps stopped right in front of the door.

Vicki peered through the door viewer to see who was standing outside. "It's Mr. Dobbs," she whispered.

"Is he the person who has been doing this?" Steve asked under his breath.

Vicki held a finger to her mouth, and simply nodded towards Steve.

Mr. Dobbs walked past and Vicki eased the door open. "Let's get out of here," she whispered. She started to push the door open, only to have someone run into it, slamming it shut.

"What's going on," Vicki asked, pushing on the door, "Something's holding it in place." Together, all three of them pushed back, but they couldn't get the door open.

"Don't try anything," Mr. Dobbs said from behind the door, "You'll never get out."

"What's holding this door," Vicki asked out loud.

"Don't do anything stupid," Mr. Dobbs told them, "I know where your friends are staying."

"They have nothing to do with this," C.J. said, "They don't know anything."

"I thought you said that they knew."

"We were lying," Vicki said.

"It doesn't matter now. I'll be getting off the ship soon and will be long gone before they find you and your friends," Mr. Dobbs' voice trailed off as he walked away.

Steve couldn't hold his disbelief any longer, "So Dobbs, my own assistant, has been stealing from the company. He's the kidnapper?"

Vicki looked surprised, and said, "I thought you knew."

"No, I had no idea," Steve said exasperated.

"Dobbs must have thought you knew he was responsible for the embezzlement, and was determined to silence you before you could tell anyone, and take the money back," Vicki said.

"Well, I couldn't exactly tell anyone if I didn't know who did it," Mr. Garcia stated.

Just then, Dobbs' voice came through the door, and surprised the captives. "So, Steve. You didn't know after all. Well, that's too bad. I would have figured you were smarter than that. I thought for sure, once Mr. Chapman accused you of embezzlement, you would have put two and two together. It should have been easy for an accountant."

"Well," Steve said, "That's kind of hard to do when all the books are at the office. I don't exactly travel around with them."

"Oh really," Dobbs said maniacally, "I do. As a matter of fact, I'll make sure the authorities find a copy of the books, with your name all over them, showing how you siphoned off all the money."

"But, I didn't. You did, Dobbs," Steve said defiantly.

"That doesn't matter now, Steve. All that matters is the evidence I will leave behind."

"Oh, by the way, Ms. Silver," Dobbs continued, "I have something you might want." He slid an object into the room. It wasn't hard for Vicki to recognize. It was a small keychain with a picture of a soldier on it. It was the mascot for Sport High School and it belonged to Joe!

CHAPTER 20

A Crook in a Dinghy

"I don't believe you," Vicki called out, "This is only a keychain. It doesn't prove anything."

"What are you talking about," C.J. whispered, "That belongs to Joe." Vicki shook her head, signifying that she knew.

"What," Mr. Dobbs voice came from outside.

"I don't believe you," Vicki repeated, "He's not that stupid. There's no way you have him."

"Have it your way," Mr. Dobbs said.

"You have no proof," Vicki called out, trying to reassure herself as well, "A keychain doesn't mean anything. You could have sneaked into his room and taken it. You got into our room last night, didn't you?" Vicki smiled as she heard him walk away, but the door was still stuck.

"He must have jammed something into it," C.J. said, "It won't budge."

"What time is it," Vicki suddenly asked her friend.

C.J. looked at her watch, "It's nine p.m. Why?" She looked at Vicki curiously.

"Joe probably went up to talk with security," Vicki said, "They should be searching the ship to find us. Let's see if we can move the door any."

"Let's just hope that they can find us," Steve Garcia spoke up, "I've been here for three days now, and I've heard no one down here but Dobbs. This area is only used for storage."

Vicki said, "You're right. They might not think to look in the storage area."

C.J. sighed, "Don't even think about it okay? Either way, we are getting out of here." She pushed at the door one more time. It still wouldn't move, "We might as well wait for them to find us."

"There has to be another way out," Vicki said.

C.J. said, "And I don't see any other door, do you?"

"No," Vicki admitted, sitting down, "I guess the only thing we can do is wait around here. I mean, it appears we're not going anywhere anytime soon."

"I know," C.J. said, "I don't like it when things like this happen."

"Right," Vicki said, "I don't get why they think locking us up will stop us, do you? We've always managed to get away."

"Maybe we can figure out what he jammed the door with," C.J. suggested, "We can try to move it at least. Maybe someone will hear the noise and let us out." She knelt by the door and tried to see through the space between the door and the lock.

"I see something," C.J. said, then she laughed, "I know what it is. He didn't do anything. It's a bar like this one." She held up the bar they had shoved in earlier, "It just wedged in. We just need to pull it out."

Vicki pushed on the door again, but it appeared to have relocked when it had been slammed shut. She sighed, "Let's get back to work, C.J."

Again they worked to pry open the door. This time Steve lent a hand. With his extra force, and C.J. working the locking mechanism with Vicki's pocketknife, they were able to push it open.

"Yes," Vicki called out. "I am glad to be out of there." Vicki let everyone step out in front of her. "Come on, let's leave before he comes back again."

Vicki suggested, "Steve, the first thing we should do is get you to security." Turning to C.J., "C.J., you take him. No detours, okay? I'm going to find Joe and the security police and show them the room."

C.J. quickly walked Mr. Garcia down the hallway and upstairs towards the security office.

Vicki closed the door and ran to find security. A few flights up, she quickly spotted Joe with a few security officers behind him, coming down the hallway.

"Hey," she yelled and waved. Joe quickly raced up when he saw her. Security followed closely behind him.

"Where were you," Joe asked, giving Vicki a huge hug, "Nobody knew where you had gone."

"Mr. Dobbs came in our room last night and kidnapped C.J. and I. He held us in a storage room a couple of flights down on the Emerald Deck."

"Catlin just told me we should check out the storage holds," Joe told her, "That's where we were headed next."

Vicki nodded quickly and then relayed the good news, "We found Steve Garcia."

"You found him?" Joe asked in astonishment.

"He was being held in the same storage room," Vicki said, "We escaped, and now C.J. is escorting Steve to the security office. And one more thing," Vicki pulled the keychain out of her pocket, "I found this."

"I didn't even realize it was gone," he said, "Where did you find it?"

"Mr. Dobbs handed it to me," she answered, "He was trying to make me believe that he had captured you, but, I knew better."

"That must have been what Dobbs was after when he broke into my room," Joe said.

He continued, "I also found something." He pulled out the necklace. Vicki smiled at Joe and slipped the necklace back on.

Vicki said, "I see you got my message."

"Where is this room," Joe asked. Vicki led the group down the corridor, and then down to the Emerald Deck.

Vicki showed them the room, "I think it's used for storage."

The security officers looked around a few moments, but the room didn't hold any clues.

"How are we going to catch Mr. Dobbs," Joe asked her after they had left.

"I don't know," she told him, "He said he was going to leave the ship. We need to find him and the evidence before he leaves."

"Don't we already have all the evidence we need. You, Steve, and C.J. are eye witnesses," Joe stated.

"Yes, but we don't have any real evidence that Dobbs is the embezzler. He plans to plant evidence implicating Steve. The real proof, of what is really going on, is in Dobbs' room. We need to get inside and grab that financial report. It's the only thing that can prove he's guilty."

Vicki and Joe walked up to Captain Maguire's office, where she found C.J. and Steve, Vicki's family was waiting there as well.

They all looked up as Vicki and Joe entered. Her mother breathed a sigh of relief upon seeing her unharmed.

Becky quietly mumbled, "Glad to see you, baby sister," then looked up at her father, "Can I go now?"

Mr. Silver looked at Becky, shook his head in disappointment, held out his hand, and said, "Only if you give me my credit card back."

Becky crossed her arms and remained where she was. Sometimes it wasn't easy having lawyers for parents. They knew just how to drive their point home.

"I see you girls found Steve," Captain Maguire said, turning his attention to Vicki and C.J. "Do you have the evidence we need to charge Mr. Dobbs?"

"I'm sorry to say, we don't," Vicki replied. The Captain looked annoyed. "But we do know where the evidence is. We just have to get to it."

"Great," the Captain said, "Where is it?"

Vicki replied, "It's with Mr. Dobbs. The problem is, we don't know where he is."

Vicki continued, "Joe and the security detail have already searched Mr. Dobbs' room, and all his stuff was gone, including the financial report that showed he was embezzling money from his own company."

C.J. interjected, "We searched the entire ship for Steve, now we have to locate Dobbs. I'm not sure I can do this again."

Vicki looked like an idea was coming to her, and she said, "We may not have to search the entire ship, just a small piece of it.

"Sir, are there any lifeboats close to the storage room where we were being held," C.J. asked. The officer, knowing the next step, bolted out of the room and headed for the elevator.

Vicki called out, "Come on guys. I think he is going to show us where Dobbs is." The group followed and piled into the elevator as well. The officer selected the Emerald Deck, where apparently all of the lifeboats were held.

When the group stepped off the elevator, there was a small crowd gathered at the edge of the railing.

"What's going on," Vicki asked, trying to see over everyone.

"Some strange man is trying to take a lifeboat," someone in the crowd said.

Vicki was surprised to see Angela Hensen peering over the rail. Jonathan and Catlin were in the crowd too.

"Angela," Vicki asked, "Do you know who took the lifeboat?"

Angela shook her head, "No, I don't."

"What does he look like?"

"He's around six feet tall with brown hair," Angela answered, "I can't see anything else." She glanced over at Vicki, "Where are you going," she asked as Vicki pushed through.

"I've got to stop this guy," Vicki told her.

Vicki received some strange looks as she pushed through. Some people didn't seem to want to move. "Get out of the way," Vicki yelled, "That man is wanted for kidnapping."

Nobody seemed to hear her though, "C.J.? Joe?" Vicki called, "See if you can get these people to move back. I need some room up here."

Her friends signaled that they would do their best and began to talk to a few people in the crowd. Apparently what they said convinced the throng to back away.

Vicki pushed through and saw Mr. Dobbs in a lifeboat, dangling about twenty feet below the deck. "Mr. Dobbs," Vicki called.

The man looked up with a start. Dobbs was very surprised to see her. "What are you doing here?"

"We escaped," Vicki told him, "The security officers know everything." She noticed a briefcase lying in the boat. "And, they might want that for evidence."

He stared at her in shock for a moment then asked, "How did you find out about that?"

"I found it in your room a few days ago," Vicki called out, "I know what you've been doing."

"What are you talking about," he asked, trying to sound innocent, "There's nothing going on."

"I know that you've been stealing money from your own company. I also know that you kidnapped Mr. Garcia when you thought he would reveal you as the crook."

"You can't prove that," he said.

"Yes, I can," Vicki said, "That briefcase holds bank statements, proving that someone has been withdrawing money from the account. I think that is pretty good evidence right there."

He glared at her for a moment, as if wondering what to do next. Then he reached into his jacket and pulled something out. It was a gun!

CHAPTER 21

Exoneration

"He's got a gun," someone in the crowd yelled, and everyone stepped back from the railing. Vicki stared Mr. Dobbs straight in the eyes.

"What are you going to do," he asked her. Just then, Joe had reached the Fiesta Deck where Dobbs was hanging. While Vicki distracted Dobbs, Joe was able to reach out and knock the gun out of his hands and into the ocean.

"You are not getting away this time," she told him. He immediately tried to drop the lifeboat into the water, but security was already there. They took over the controls used to lower the lifeboat, and arrested Dobbs.

Vicki made it to the deck where the lifeboat was held. She reached in and grabbed the briefcase. And, after finding the right key, opened it. She handed the contents to security.

"This is all the evidence you'll need to prove that Dobbs was behind the embezzlement. And, C.J., Steve, and I can attest to the fact that Dobbs kidnapped us."

Suddenly, Vicki noticed a man watching them from the crowd. She turned to Joe and pointed to him, "Does he look familiar to you?"

Joe casually glanced over, "Yeah, it looks like the other man who was talking with Steve at the club. What's he doing here?" The man was tall with black hair. Vicki and Joe walked over.

"Excuse me," Vicki said, "Can I ask you something? Weren't you talking with Mr. Garcia at the club a few days ago?"

The man glanced up, as if surprised, "Yes, I was. How did you know about that?"

"We were there when it happened," Vicki answered, "I remember you saying something about money being skimmed off the top, and Mr. Garcia was the only one with access. Can you tell me what were you talking to him about?"

"I'm Steve's boss, Mark Chapman," the man replied, "I'm the President of AGM. And, who are you?"

"My friends and I were helping the Captain investigate Mr. Garcia's disappearance," Vicki replied. "We've been looking into Mr. Garcia's disappearance. With the help of these security officers, we just apprehended Mr. Dobbs, who I believe also works for AGM. We have evidence that he has been embezzling money from your company."

"I thought Steve was the embezzler. I feel terrible that I accused him. Steve always insisted he wasn't involved."

"Was that what you meant when you said Steve owed you," Joe cut in, "You wanted the money back, even though Steve never had it in the first place. What made you suspect him?"

"He's the CFO of the company," he answered, "He had the easiest access to the money. We never suspected Mr. Dobbs of doing something like this."

Mr. Chapman asked, "Where is Steve now? Is he okay?"

"Yes, sir. He's fine now. But, he's been through quite an ordeal. I believe he's upstairs at the security office."

CHAPTER 22

The Reunion

Susan sat in her room, hoping that word would come soon concerning her fiancé. The cruise was ending the next day and Susan had heard nothing since that morning when she had been informed of Vicki and C.J.'s disappearance. She refused to leave the room until she received news, whether good or bad.

She opened the jewelry box that held her engagement ring and hesitantly placed it on her left ring finger. She didn't generally like to wear it out, as she had a fear of leaving it somewhere and losing it. But right now, on a small level, wearing it made her feel like Steve was there with her.

Susan was disturbed from her thoughts by a frantic knocking on her door. Hoping that it was news about Steve, Susan raced to answer it. Upon seeing who was on the other side, the hand holding onto the doorknob immediately joined the other as she flung them around Steve's neck. Steve stumbled back several steps before regaining his balance and returning the gesture.

Susan didn't know whether she was laughing or crying. All she was aware of was that her cheeks hurt from smiling so much and she was shaking uncontrollably. Her hands gripped onto the back of his shirt, sure to leave wrinkles in their wake.

"Steve," Susan cried, "Are you okay? Where have you been? I have so many questions."

Steve smiled in reply, "I'm fine dear. These young ladies you hired came and found me. They also exposed Mr. Dobbs as the man behind the embezzlement at the office. So, I'm cleared of any wrong doing, and Mr. Dobbs will be put away for a long time.

Susan saw Vicki and C.J. awkwardly watching the scene. They appeared to be attempting to find a quick exit without drawing attention to themselves.

"Girls," Susan called to them. She approached Vicki and C.J., hugging each of them in turn, though Vicki tensed at the close contact, "I don't know how to thank you for all you've done."

"We were just glad to help," Vicki answered with a smile.

"Well, we'll leave you two alone," C.J. remarked, obviously still feeling awkward about invading Steve and Susan's celebratory reunion. Everyone wanted to give the newly reunited couple as much space as they desired.

Later that day, after Mr. Dobbs had been handed over to the Coast Guard, the final pieces of the puzzle were put together.

During their questioning, they determined that Mr. Dobbs was solely responsible for all of the kidnappings and break-ins onboard. The pocketknife and prints that Vicki found in Susan's room matched Dobbs.

They also matched the suicide note with the paper and printers used in the computer center, where the attendants remembered seeing Dobbs the first day of the cruise.

As far as Steve, Dobbs surprised him at his cabin door, by assaulting him, and then knocking him out with a blow to the head. Dobbs initially held Steve in room E three-twenty-seven, after he got the room quarantined by complaining it made him sick. Dobbs quickly decided though, he couldn't run the risk of passengers in the adjoining rooms hearing Steve after he woke up, so he began searching for a new location.

Mr. Dobbs then acquired the key to the storage hold by breaking into the Purser's office. He selected the storage area on the Emerald Deck, because that deck is where all the lifeboats are stored. And, in his mind, would make for an easy exit.

It appears Dobbs didn't intend to actually harm Steve, or the girls. He planted the suicide note in Steve's room to keep the ship's security team from investigating further. And, he only held the girls long enough to attempt his escape.

Fortunately for everyone, it isn't easy to lower a lifeboat by oneself. And, Dobbs might have attempted it earlier, but the idea of operating a lifeboat on the open sea was daunting. So, Dobbs waited until they were closest to the shoreline. They were practically in Quebec City harbor before he finally decided to attempt to launch it.

The ship's security team ran across four pages of a financial report that Dobbs planted in Steve's gym bag, along with the ten thousand dollars. Once they put the pieces of the report back together, it turned out Dobbs had actually embezzled over two hundred and fifty thousand dollars, and not just the one hundred and thirty that was thought earlier.

Most of Dobbs' crimes were committed while the ship sailed in territorial waters of various countries. But, maritime law says the country under whose flag the ship sails has jurisdiction. And, since the Crystal Palace sails under the American flag, Dobbs' would be facing a U.S. court for his crimes.

CHAPTER 23

Forever

Steve and Susan decided to get married right away, while still onboard the 'Crystal Palace'. Susan asked Vicki, C.J., and the rest of the group to attend the wedding the next morning.

The wedding took place in the chapel, just the way they had planned. Chaplain Nahalea was very happy to pull out all the decorations again, and prepare the chapel for a proper ceremony.

Natasha was the maid of honor, and Vicki, C.J. and Catlin were last minute bridesmaids. Joe was the honorary best man, since Steve's brother was no longer on board. Vicki's parents, Becky, and several other friends and acquaintances were among the guests witnessing the happy occasion.

The wedding march began, and the crowd rose to greet the coming bride. The double doors parted, to reveal a beautiful Susan Morrow. Her dress was an elegant shimmery white, and detailed with pearls.

Steve's heart pounded in his chest, as he couldn't believe how beautiful she looked. The time was finally here. It seemed that God had brought them together so long ago, and now they would be together forever.

Susan was escorted down the aisle by Steve's boss, Mark Chapman, who walked her to the front, and placed her hand in Steve's.

Chaplain Nahalea began with these words, "Family and friends, and honored guests, we welcome you here today, to witness the joining together of Steve Garcia and Susan Morrow, in holy matrimony."

"Steve and Susan, the past few days have been harrowing times, times that tried your faith. But, here you are, safe in each other's presence, ready to receive God's blessings on your marriage together."

"May you always remember, that no matter what may come against you, if you will hold fast to your faith, God will pull you through."

The Chaplain turned to Joe, and motioned for the ring. Joe fumbled a bit in his pocket, but eventually he found the little jewelry box covered in dark blue velvet. He pulled the ring from its case, and carefully placed it in the Chaplain's hand.

Chaplain Nahalea first looked closely at the inside of the ring, and then turned to the guests. "Steve and Susan have placed a very special inscription on the inside of their rings. It reads as follows, 'SM plus SG plus G equals 4E'."

He continued, "If you were to see this inscription, not knowing what it meant, you might wonder, is it a secret covert message shared between spies. Or, maybe it could be a formula for some scientific breakthrough."

"Well, it is a special message, and it is a formula, but not the kind you think. What it actually means is this, 'SM' Susan Morrow, plus 'SG', Steven Garcia, plus 'G,' God, equals '4E', Forever."

The crowd reacted with smiles and muffled exchanges.

"That's an important message for all of us. No two people on earth are completely compatible. At best, we put up with each other's faults. And at worst, we bicker over petty differences. But, when we acknowledge that the God who created the institution of marriage can and will help you to succeed at marriage, then we can expect it will last '4E' · forever."

Next, the chaplain invited the couple to join hands. They exchanged their rings and vows. And then, finally, they were invited to share in their first kiss, which they did with all their might. To the point that the sensibilities of some of the older guests were just a little ruffled.

"Ladies and gentlemen, I now present to you, Mr. and Mrs. Steve Garcia," said Chaplain Nahalea.

The music rose, inviting the crowd to their feet again, as the newly married couple walked down the aisle. This was the start of their new lives together.

The reception followed immediately thereafter, and was a joyous occasion. Everyone congratulated the newlyweds, and tried their best not to delve into the details of the last few days. The chef had prepared a beautiful multi-tiered cake, decorated with blue sea horses and tan starfish.

When it came time to toss the bouquet, Susan decided to walk up to the next level, to the Emerald Deck. A small crowd of young ladies gathered on the deck below, awaiting the prize. Vicki wasn't about to get caught up in such a display, but C.J., Catlin, and even Becky were game for a little fun.

Finally, Susan tossed the bouquet to the group below, where her friend Natasha scrambled to catch it before it could go over the railing. Unfortunately for Natasha, Catlin was a little more aggressive, and snatched the prize amid the fury of flailing arms.

Everyone who knew Catlin, was not surprised to see her walk away with the symbol of impeding nuptials. They only wondered, of all her suitors, which young man would eventually have her as prize.

The celebration lasted a few hours, and then each of the guests departed, after giving the couple one more heart felt 'congratulations'.

Considering their ordeal, the Captain had upgraded the couple's room to a Balcony Suite, where the two could spend their last few days of the cruise together in luxury.

CHAPTER 24

Two Tickets to Paradise

Vicki and her friends stood in the Captain's office, as the Captain stood behind his desk, "I want to thank you all for helping out with this case," he began, "I admit that I didn't quite trust you at first, but I'm glad that you caught this kidnapper." He paused for a second.

"And," Vicki asked, "What were you going to say next?" They all looked at the Captain.

"And the Coast Guard wants me to thank you as well," he finally said, "I wanted to give you these." He handed each of them an envelope with tickets inside, "They are tickets to come back anytime. There's two tickets for each of you."

"We would like to try another cruise. As long as you promise there won't be another mystery," C.J. asked, "Next time, I'll jump overboard if there is."

"I don't know if I could make that kind of promise," the Captain said with a smile, "but I hope not."

"Captain," Vicki said, "We are glad we could help. Susan and Steve are a great couple, and they deserve the chance for a good life together."

"I agree," he said, "I'm just glad that it's over with. A lot of the passengers were getting suspicious of all these new workers running around. It's time things get back to normal." The group smiled.

Later that day, the ship finally arrived at Quebec City. Vicki, her friends, and family all took off on the most anticipated part of their journey. Their cruise coincided with the biggest event held in Quebec City each year. It was called Festival d'ete de Quebec, or Quebec City Summer Festival.

The group arrived at the main outdoor arena called the Plains of Abraham. This is a large plateau along the St. Lawrence River where a significant battle was fought in 1759. Joe was amazed at the fortifications that still stand along the river.

During the festival, this area is host to Francophone music, which is a collection of music from French speaking nations from around the world. Vicki and her friends were mainly there to listen to some of the more modern world music.

After some time at the musical venues, the group made its way to the downtown district, where they were sure to run into street performers, known as 'arts de la rue'. There were amazing musicians, comedians, and even mimes. One man could swallow a sword the length of his arm, and then blow fire from his mouth ten feet into the air. It was all a little too surreal after being cooped up on the ship the past five days.

That evening, Vicki's parents insisted everyone attend the Grand Theater, in hopes their two daughters would gain some appreciation for the classical music presented. But, for these teenage girls, that would be an uphill battle.

The evening ended with fire works, and the group thought it best to view them from onboard. The reflection in the bay made an amazing spectacle. Vicki allowed the display to wash over her, and help her shake off all the former feelings from the trip thus far.

This would be a great way to remember their cruise.

When the trip ended, Vicki and her family and friends were among the first passengers off.

They found their way out front where Vicki, Catlin, Joe and C.J. met at her car. "Hey guys," they heard a voice say nearby. Susan and Steve were making their way over to them. "Thank you again, for everything."

"Thank you," said Vicki. "And again, congratulations."

"Thanks again," Steve said, "We called Susan's father a moment ago. When he heard what happened, he was so happy that Susan was safe."

After talking a while, the four explained that they had to be leaving.

"Well, we should get going, too," Susan remarked, "We shouldn't keep my father waiting." The two walked off. Vicki and her friends watched as they left.

"I'm glad that's over," Catlin said with a relieved sigh, "But next time, could I just sit back and watch, instead of being in the line of fire?"

"Sure, Catlin," Joe teased, "Next time, we'll put you on stake out duty."

"I hate stake outs," Catlin growled. "Unless I get to sit next to a cute guy."

The rest of the gang laughed, except for Vicki, who just groaned and rolled her eyes. "Come on, guys. Let's go to the city pool. There were four pools and two hot tubs on that ship, and I didn't even get my big toe wet!"

With shouts of approval, they piled into Vicki's red convertible and pulled away from the dock, music blasting. For just those few moments, everything seemed normal again.

"Wait!" Vicki said, "We have to go back. I forgot to try the rock climbing wall."

The group yelled, "Keep driving!"

Printed in the United States
203656BV00001B/1-105/P

9 780980 186116